THE
LAST KEY

A Baker Girls Romance

BETHANY MONACO SMITH

ABOUT THE LAST KEY

The Last Key is the second book in the Baker Girls interconnected standalone series. All books in the series can be read as standalone novels.
The Last Key is a low angst, small town rom-com featuring two lifelong besties, Devon and Kennedy, who have been denying their feelings for each other for the sake of their friendship. *The Last Key* is full of sexy teasing, hilarious banter, and plenty of steamy and swoony moments.
Ready to fall in love with Devon and Kennedy?

AUTHOR'S NOTE

This story was originally published as part of the Brighton High School Reunion shared world, which featured twelve stories set in the same world, with occasional crossover characters. You don't need to have read any of those books to enjoy this one as they are all complete standalones. This version is primarily the same as the original version, only minor details have been changed for continuity, in addition to a new cover and interior formatting. If you are interested in reading the rest of the shared world... some books may have been removed, changed, or updated. You can find more information about the individual books from the authors involved: Em Torrey, M. Bonnet, Shayna Astor, Poppy Jacobson, Bre Rose, Cassie Lein, Aly Beck, Lyric Nicole, MK Robert, Raja Savage, and Whitnay Edes.

MEET THE CHARACTERS

The besties who totally aren't in love:

- Devon McGregor
- Kennedy Baker

The Baker Girls family/friends:

- Justin Ayers
- Frannie Baker
- Hallie Baker
- Mark Abbott
- Ryan Hardison (Hardy)
- Brian Ackley

The Brighton crew:

- Gladys Tipton
- Sharon & Lon McGregor
- Claire Daniels
- Lily Brant

TRIGGER WARNING

If you're looking for possible triggers in this book, this page is for you. If you're not, you can skip this page and dive into the story.

trigger warnings may contain plot spoilers

As a lighthearted read, I tried my best to keep this one as trigger-free as possible. The following things are mentioned/discussed: caring for chronically ill parents—including rheumatoid arthritis & multiple sclerosis, brief depiction of misogynistic boss

Any updates or changes to this information can be found at bethanymonacosmith.com/triggers

To Cassie
At least someone is organized

BACK
THEN

Kennedy

MOVING SUCKS.

This morning I was at home in Manhattan. Sure, my bedroom was empty as I sat on the floor, but it was still home. Then I had to say goodbye to my cousins, Frannie and Hallie, who are more like my sisters. We stood in a group hug, crying, until my parents dragged me to the car so we could catch our stupid flight out here.

It's not fair.

And it sucks.

Everything sucks.

Now I'm on the other side of the country in some suburb of San Francisco. *Brighton*. All because my dad got some dream job in San Francisco. How is it possibly the dream if you have to leave your family behind?

Frannie and Hallie lived right next door to us because their mom is my mom's sister and their dad is my dad's brother. We were one big, crazy family. Now we're fractured on opposite coasts of this stupid country. I hate it.

I'm about to turn twelve and I have to start at a new middle school, in case starting at one wasn't horrible enough this year. I don't even know what to expect from California kids. Are they hippies who say 'dude' all the time or something?

"Hey, honey," Dad says, walking out onto the back porch. The floorboards creak beneath his feet.

"What do you want?"

"I found your soccer ball. I thought maybe you'd like to have it for the backyard. We finally have space for you to play at home."

"Yeah, but I have no one to play with, so it doesn't really matter."

He sighs and sits down next to me. I turn my body away from him. *He* is the one who ruined everything.

"Honey, I know you're mad at me. But I promise, in time, you'll like it here. And I'll make sure Frannie and Hallie come visit. They can even stay for a couple of months in the summer."

Great. Eight months from now.

"Whatever. Can I call them tonight at least?"

"Sure."

He sits for a moment longer, then squeezes my shoulder and stands, leaving the soccer ball sitting next to me.

Rather than touch my soccer ball, I continue sitting on the back steps, elbows on my knees and chin resting on my hands. Leaves rustle through the trees bordering the back of our property. Birds chirp and bugs whizz around me.

Ugh. It's so quiet here. And boring. We're at the end of a dead-end road. *Apple Lane.*

Nothing to see besides grass and woods. In New York, I could go up to the storage space on the third floor and look out the windows and see traffic rolling through the city, police cars and ambulances rushing through the crowded streets, and people out walking. The sounds to go along with all that echoed through the house. Trains in the distance. Now it's just silence.

Growling, I grab my soccer ball and run for the back of the yard, drop the ball in front of me, and kick it hard against the black chain-link fence. *Clang.* I chase after the ball and kick it at the fence again. And again and again, taking out all my frustration on this stupid fence. Stupid, lonely, perfect yard.

I kick and kick and kick, letting out all my anger and pain. Tears stream down my cheeks, and I kick harder, then drop to the ground, wiping my cheeks as I sniffle.

"Wow. You can really kick," comes a voice from behind me.

I turn and see a gangly boy with curly blond hair and the greenest eyes I've ever seen.

I sniff again and turn back to the fence.

A moment later, he's sitting next to me.

"I'm Devon. I live next door," he says softly.

"Kennedy," I sniff.

"Just moved in?"

I nod.

"Don't want to be here?"

"Nope. I left my home and my life and my cousins—they're my best friends. Now I have to start all over. I'm angry. I'm lonely. And this just... sucks."

"Well, you can be angry, but you don't have to be lonely."

My eyes shift toward him. "No?"

He looks out at the woods. "Nope. I've been looking for a good best friend. You seem nice enough. You like soccer. And you don't mind crying in front of me, which means you don't care about appearances like most girls in my school do." He rolls his eyes. "Actually, how do you feel about camping?"

I turn so I'm partially facing him. "I like camping. My dad and my uncle would take my cousins and me on a camping trip every summer. Tents. Not a camper."

He smiles and nods approvingly. "Yep. We can definitely be best friends. We can camp in my backyard. We have a firepit and we can roast marshmallows."

"Can we drink hot cocoa, too?"

"Sure."

"Okay, then."

"Okay, then." He nods toward my ball. "Wanna play?"

I look at him for a moment, and for the first time since we left our house this morning, I smile.

"Yeah. I'd like that."

He stands and offers me his hand, pulling me from the ground.

Then he smiles, and it's this cute, troublesome half-smile.

And some part of me knows we're going to be friends for a long time.

Maybe, just *maybe,* this place won't suck quite as much now.

Devon

"I DIDN'T THINK it was going to rain this much," I say, looking up at the top of the tent, grateful I put on both the rain fly *and* a tarp. I thought it might be too much, at the time, but I guess not.

"I know. Normally, I love the rain, but I'm freezing," Kennedy says.

She's in her sleeping bag but still shivering.

We didn't bring any extra blankets this time, and neither of us wants to run out in the rain if we don't have to.

"Come here," I say, unzipping the side of my sleeping bag. "Bring yours with you."

She climbs out of the sleeping bag and no wonder she's freezing. She's wearing the skimpiest little sleep shorts I've ever seen.

Crap.

I can barely control my boners on a good day. Forget when I'm alone with Kennedy. Now she's in tiny shorts. And snuggling against me. Crap. Crap. Crap.

"What do you want me to do?" she asks.

"What?" I choke out.

"With my sleeping bag," she says.

"Oh." *Right.* Because Kennedy does not have feelings for me. Despite what I feel for her—a massive crush and epic horniness.

"Stand up for a second," I tell her. I stand too, then unzip her sleeping bag and tuck the bottom underneath mine. We both settle back in my sleeping bag, then pull the top of hers over us.

She leans against me and wraps her arm around my waist.

Do not get hard. Don't do it, I command my dick.

"Thanks for keeping me warm."

"Always," I say, trying not to sound as worked up as I am.

She twirls her finger over my abs.

Yep, there it is.

At least it's only a semi and not a full hard-on.

This is fine. As long as I stay where I am and she stays where she is, she won't feel it.

"I love the sound of the rain," she whispers.

"It's peaceful," I agree, rubbing my hand down her back.

Moments like this make me question if I'm wrong about how she feels about me, but then I think back to last year.

It was my fourteenth birthday party, and I'd invited a bunch of kids from school. I didn't really want to do anything big, but since my mother knows so many of theirs, I invited them all anyway. My parents were cool about it all and let me have a semi-supervised party at Brighton Manor—the inn my mother's family has owned and operated for several generations.

A group of girls got the idea to play spin the bottle, and most of the guys, eager to be kissed, agreed. Kennedy and I went to the pantry looking for a bottle to use, and she asked me if I really wanted to play.

My heart was pounding as I spun around and looked at her.

"There's only one girl I really want to kiss."

"Oh. Who?"

I raised my eyebrows as I stared at her.

Her eyes widened as I moved closer, but she didn't stop me. My hand was on her arm and my gaze was on her lips when the group of girls appeared at the doorway asking if we'd found a bottle yet.

Kennedy yanked her arm away, grabbed a glass bottle of ketchup, shoved it in one of the girl's hands, and walked away. She wouldn't play with us. Once the game got started, I didn't even want to play because all the girls were purposely trying to land on me. I just wanted a fun night with my best friend, but I'd scared her. That night, I made a promise to myself not to try it again, but it didn't make my feelings disappear.

Moments like this, though, are confusing. Her fingers are now at the hem of my shirt, brushing the skin above my waistband.

"Kennedy?"

"Hm?" She tilts her head up to look at my face.

"Want to go to homecoming with me?"

Maybe I'm breaking my promise to myself by asking her, but there's no one else I want to go with.

"Really? You want to go with me?" she asks, surprised.

"Yeah. Of course. We always have fun together."

"Fun. Right." Now she sounds disappointed, and I don't understand why.

I think for a second, then carefully roll onto my side, being sure to keep my hips pulled back away from her.

"Is fun a bad thing?"

"No..." She pulls her bottom lip between her teeth, and I almost groan. "I just... there are so many other girls you could go with. I saw at least one show you her cleavage this week."

I roll my eyes at that.

"Yeah. And that's *not* what I find attractive."

"You don't like boobs?" she teases.

Don't look at her boobs. Don't look at her boobs.

Keeping my eyes steady on her face, I say, "I do. But..." *But what? I like your boobs?* "I don't want the girls who are shoving their boobs in my face." I clear my throat. "You're the one I'd rather go with. If you ever let me stop begging."

She laughs. "Okay, then. I'd love to go with you."

"Good."

I flop onto my back again, and she drapes her arm over my chest and nestles her head against my shoulder. Then I switch off the LED lantern sitting next to us. As she slowly drifts off, I softly kiss her head and revel in this moment since I'm not sure I'll ever get more than this.

PRESENT
DAY

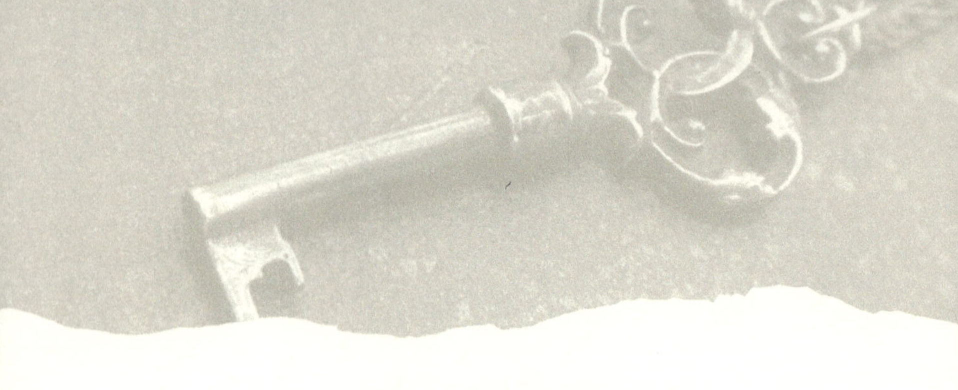

CHAPTER ONE

MONItroD

MONDAY

Kennedy

"YOU JUST HIRED three new people last month and now you're laying *me* off? I've been here for nine months," I fruitlessly argue with my department head, who I can't stand.

From day one, he's been a disgusting misogynist, frequently pitting women in the office against each other like there's no role for women in journalism. *Fuck this guy.* Except for the fact I thought I finally hit career status. Instead of working freelance jobs or for tiny papers or websites—where I got laid off a few months after getting hired—I'd finally made it to one of the bigger online news sites. Long hours and shitty pay got me here, and I thought I was on the right track, not on track for another layoff. Even though this isn't a layoff. It's an underhanded way of pushing me out for someone he likes better.

"I'm sorry, Ms. Baker, but it's not just about the length of time you've worked here. It's also about overall performance—"

"Was there a problem with my performance? All my review meetings with my editor have been positive."

My editor, who is my immediate boss, has been extremely supportive of my career. He does his best to give me interesting pieces covering dramatic TV series, movies, and books. Rather than recapping the stories, I dove deep into how they played into the viewers' or readers' emotions and the meat of the storyline, all while connecting with my readers. My editor said our likes and comments on the articles about those shows had grown since I'd taken over. He said I had a way of reaching people and drawing them into the depth of a story, and would try to get me more human interest stories—my personal preference and where I think I shine.

I've been told for years I have a natural way of connecting with people, and it translates into my writing.

But this jackass doesn't care.

Mr. Hunt looks at me shrewdly. "Frankly, it comes down to your professionalism, Ms. Baker."

Ah yes. Over the nine months I've worked here, he's harped on me several times for not looking "professional" enough. I wear dress leggings, flats or heels, and dressy tops that cover up everything. That's the real problem. I don't wear low-cut shirts or skirts that hug my ass. He wants the women who work for him to dress the way *he* wants. I'm ashamed to say that after several comments about the length of my hair and how "ratty" it looked—despite it always being styled and often tucked back in a bun—I cut my hair into a bob. The approving and incredibly demeaning look he gave me when I walked into the office after that made me want to vomit.

I wouldn't have stuck around in this job if he were my immediate boss or someone I had to deal with on a daily basis. Or if it hadn't felt like I was settling into my career. I know I've done good work here, and I know this is bullshit.

So, I do what any good journalist would do. I pull out my notepad.

"What are you doing?" he asks.

"Writing down some notes." I look up at him innocently. "How can I improve if I don't take note of the problem?"

He clears his throat. "I see."

"So, you've noted my performance is fine, correct?"

"Yes. Well, generally speaking, your reviews from your editor have been—fine."

"Great. And you said the length of time I've worked here doesn't play a role?"

"Well, it's a factor, but not the determining one."

"Okay." I look up at him. "And what would you say was the biggest issue with my professionalism?"

He pulls at his shirt collar. "Well, it's not..." He huffs loudly. "Your outward appearance doesn't meet the standards set by this department."

I make a point of repeating every word back as I write it down. Then I look at him with sincerity. Well, fake sincerity, but he doesn't need to know that. "Thank you for the chance to work here. I learned a lot."

"Of course. No hard feelings. The economy is just," he flits his hand back and forth in the air.

"Sure."

I turn to leave and he calls after me. "Don't forget to leave your badge with HR."

Oh, I'll leave plenty with HR.

When I walk back to my desk to collect my things, I'm feeling confident, until I feel the heat of my colleagues' gazes burning into me.

Okay, no matter how ridiculous this all is, it's still embarrassing to be forced to pack up the five whole things I have at my desk while everyone stares. Three pictures. One with my parents, one with Hallie and Frannie, and one with Devon. A pack of my favorite pens and a package of notepads.

After throwing them all into my large purse, I make my way

toward the elevator with my head held high. I'm almost home free when my boss waves me into his office.

"I'm so sorry about this, Kennedy. For whatever it's worth, I fought for you. You have talent plenty of people on staff would kill for. If you need any references or anything related to this job, please let me know. I'm happy to sing your praises."

"Thanks. I appreciate it," I say softly, my skin burning with embarrassment and anger. I just want to get out of here. *And chat with HR.*

"Oh, here," he says, grabbing a gift card off his desk and shoving it in my hand. "I know it's not much, but..." He runs a hand through his hair like he realizes how stupid it is.

"Thanks. Take care," I say before scurrying out of the office and down the hall.

Once I'm safely in the elevator, I look down at the card he gave me. Ten bucks for the coffee place down the street.

Phenomenal.

The doors open to the first floor, and I stride out, focused on reclaiming my confidence. I pull out my notepad and remember the look on Mr. Hunt's face as I took those notes. He knows what he did. What he doesn't realize is I'm scrappy and don't go down without a fight.

Walking into HR, I wait until one of the reps is available to talk, then I hand over my badge, the notes I took, and file a complaint against Mr. Hunt. Maybe it'll look bad to them, but I've got to give it a shot. At the very least, it might lay the groundwork if someone else files a complaint in the future.

Once I've finished, I walk out of HR, out of the building, and go straight to the nearby coffee shop to spend my pathetic gift card.

"DAMN, GIRL. YOU'RE BADASS," Ryan Hardison—who we all call Hardy—says, waggling his thick black eyebrows at me and raising a glass in my honor.

"I'll second that," my cousin and roommate Hallie says, the liquid in her glass sloshing a bit.

"Seriously. You want a job with the Bandits?" Hardy asks. "I've got connections." Hardy is a wide receiver for the New York Bandits—currently the top team in New York and ranked third in the NFL.

Yes, I'm friends with a professional football player. Several, actually. Only because my cousin Frannie had the hilariously good fortune to sit next to their quarterback, Mark Abbott, on a plane a few months back. She was panicking, he calmed her down, she had no idea who he was, they ended up at the same resort, and well, now we're all sitting together in his swanky condo.

Though Frannie lives upstate in the small, idyllic town of Ida now, she and Mark are down here for the weekend.

"Woo, working the Bandits press room and cleaning up all your messes. Sounds fun," I say, chomping on some General Tso's.

"Hey, we're not all troublemakers," Brian Ackley, a massive lineman who looks menacing but is actually a big cuddly marshmallow, says.

"I second that," Mark says, sitting down next to Frannie and pulling her close. They're annoyingly adorable together. "Plus the pay is incredible."

"I'll keep it in mind," I say, throwing back the rest of my drink and slurping down some lo mein.

I'm open to a new path, I'm just not sure that's the right one.

Smash a window.

The words have been ringing in my brain all day. That's what Devon always tells me I need to do.

My mother—forever a hardass optimist—tells me to pull myself up by the bootstraps and move on to the next thing. *It's always the last key that opens the door,* she loves to say—a.k.a. keep trying and don't give up. Easy for her to say. I can't even find my keys most days.

Devon, on the other hand, would tell me I need to blaze my own trail. I thought I fucking was this time. Maybe I've been treading down the same worn path I have been for years. Maybe I do need to jump in the weeds and make my own path, but the problem is, I don't even know which direction I want that path to go.

I need a break. And to clear my head. I need my best friend.

Looking around the room, I'm grateful to the crazy people sitting on the floor around a coffee table with me, but I miss Devon. Frannie and Hallie know me better than almost anyone. They know when I need tough love and they know when to hand me a pint of ice cream. But since the moment I met him, no one has calmed me down like Devon does. Somehow, he knows exactly what I need. A hug, pizza, getting the anger out, crying, whatever I need, he's there.

My friendship with him was the best thing that came out of moving to Brighton. After high school, we moved to Chicago together for college, then he moved back to New York with me for a couple of years. He was working as a model at the time and was living with our friend, Justin, who we met in Chicago and is also a model. I was living with Frannie and Hallie. The five of us had the best times together, but then Justin moved back down to Georgia where he's from. Frannie moved up to Ida. Then Devon moved back to Brighton when his dad was diagnosed with MS. Since then, we only see each other a couple of times a year, usually for joint vacations. I haven't even been back to Brighton since graduation. That all changes next week, though. In ten days, I'm headed back for my ten-year high school reunion.

I don't want to wait ten days.

And why the hell should I? It's not like I'm going to find a new job in that time. Two weeks with my best friend instead of four days? Hell yes.

That's it. Decision made.

Without another thought, I grab my phone off the table in front of me, open my travel app, and book a redeye to San Francisco tonight.

"Oh, she's got that look in her eye," Frannie says.

I set my phone down and look at her. "What look?"

"The *watch out world* look," Hallie says, amused. "What were you doing just now?"

I shrug and smile. "Booking a flight to San Fran. Tonight."

"Ooh, gonna go see the hot bestie early?" Hardy asks.

"Aw, you think he's hot? I'll be sure to tell him that Ryan Hardison has a *hard-on* for him."

"Hey now, I didn't say *that*. Not like he's on my list."

"I'd assume not, since you're straight," I say.

"Excuse me, I can appreciate a hot man. For your information, I have Henry Cavil on that list. But only if he's in his Geralt costume." Hardy shivers. "Mm."

"This has taken a turn," Mark says in bewilderment.

"Right. Back to the point. Are you finally going to jump Devon's bones?" Hallie asks, grinning like the Cheshire Cat. She categorically loathes love for herself, but for everyone else, she's ready to plan a wedding.

"Or even mention how you feel about him?" Frannie asks innocently.

Hard no.

I don't bother saying we're just friends because I know it'll achieve nothing. They all know I have feelings for Devon, but I put them away a long time ago. As soon as I realized every girl in school wanted him and he could have whoever he wanted, I put him in the friendzone, unwilling to risk a rejection from him that could destroy our friendship. It's too important to me, and it has been since the beginning.

It was the right decision. Nothing has ever happened between us. I went on to successfully date and hook up with other guys. Maybe not *successfully* since I've been single for more than a year, but dating other people was never an issue, and we were able to bring boyfriends and girlfriends around each other without any jealousy. Outward jealousy, at least. I've always been a little jealous of the girls he dates, but I get over it by leaning into our friendship. When we're together, it's easy to focus on that.

It's harder when we're apart. I'm single. My mind wanders. To Devon.

Have I fantasized what it would be like to be with him?

Yes.

But have I touched myself dreaming of his lean muscular chest rolling over mine?

Also yes.

What can I say? A girl has needs. And as long as I don't think about those things when I'm around him, I'll be fine.

"I'm not telling him anything because there's nothing to tell. We're friends. And that's all I need us to be."

"But you *want* more," Hallie presses.

Sighing, I open my mouth to respond, but Brian speaks first.

"Let it go. How many of you have ever had feelings for someone close to you?" Everyone looks around, but no one says anything. "Exactly my point," he continues. "It's not easy to risk everything with a friend and possibly lose an important relationship. Give her shit about whatever else you want, but let this go."

"Thanks," I say softly.

He nods as he tips his beer bottle back and takes a drink.

Hardy is looking at Brian out of the corner of his eye, like he's trying to figure out who Brian's talking about. He's never mentioned anyone, but he seems sad about it.

I get it.

Which is why I'm not stepping close to that line.

I'm going to Brighton, but I'm staying in the friendzone.

Some windows you just can't smash.

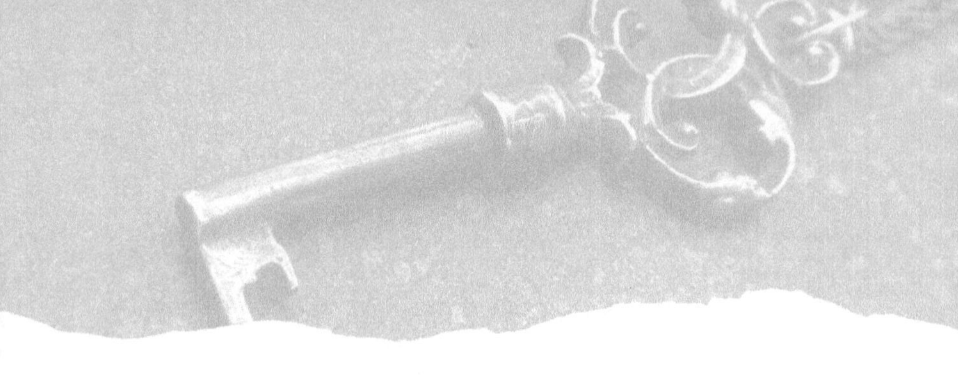

CHAPTER TWO

TUESDAY

Devon

I CAN'T SLEEP.

Other than in my teen years when sleeping was a full-time job, I've always been a light sleeper. A weird dream, a small sound, or my brain's inability to shut up will drag me out of sleep, especially in the bleary-eyed morning hours.

Fuck it.

It's almost five. That's a reasonable waking hour.

If you're ninety-two.

Or one of those crazy people who gets up before the sun to run.

I like staying in shape, but the thought of getting out of bed to run when it's still dark is a hard no for me.

But coffee and staring at a computer are doable, so I throw the covers off, slide my feet into my slippers, grab a sweatshirt, and head downstairs.

My first stop is the simple espresso maker I have. I throw a pod in, then grab the milk from the fridge and pour a cup in the steamer/frother combination and turn it on. A few minutes and some toffee syrup later, and I have my favorite latte.

After warming up a slice of chocolate chip banana bread, I grab my laptop and sit down at the kitchen island.

Damn, Gladys makes the best banana bread ever.

Gladys Tipton is the innkeeper at Brighton Manor and has been for most of my life. She's in her midfifties, sweet and motherly, and always brings baked goods to work. She's like a second mother to me, and I wouldn't be able to run the place without her.

I moved back to Brighton a few years ago to take over Brighton Manor operations from my parents after my dad was diagnosed with MS. My mother has been dealing with rheumatoid arthritis for half of my life, so with my dad's diagnosis, anything more than living became too much for them. My parents are only in their midfifties, so it's hard to see them struggle like this so soon.

Since getting up and down the stairs of this house was tough for both of them, I bought the place—for much less than they should've sold it to me—and they moved into an apartment building in downtown Brighton with an elevator and a concierge service.

When I packed up and moved back here, I was a son doing his duty. I love my parents, they're incredible people, and as their only son, I wasn't going to leave them alone to deal with this. That doesn't mean I was excited about it.

I'd spent the previous years living in Chicago and New York with Kennedy and our friend Justin, and we'd had a lot of fun. While I was tired of modeling, it got me through my college years. As I grew older, it began feeling like an invasion of my privacy. Social media was taking over my life. I didn't like it, but I was still loving my life in the city with my best friends. I'd accepted a job as a modeling agent, putting the business degree I'd earned in college to use. I traveled when I could, and was, as they say, living my best life.

Then it all changed. I thought I'd go crazy living in Brighton, and don't get me wrong, life is slower here than in a big city, but not as slow as I thought it would be. I was surprised I didn't feel any resentment and settled in here easily. With San Francisco nearby, I have access to everything I could want or need. Minus one thing. Kennedy.

Yep, that's me. The sad sack who's hung up on his best friend, despite the fact she has never been interested in having more with me. As far as I know, at least. For a moment, when we were young, I thought it might happen, but she shut me down before I could even kiss her, and since then, nothing romantic has ever happened. We're close. Maybe even more affectionate than two best friends should be—we cuddle and sometimes share the same bed, but never once have we inappropriately touched each other or even kissed.

God, what I wouldn't give to taste those plush pink lips. Other parts of her, too. Bury myself deep inside her until she's screaming my name.

At that thought, my cock comes alive.

Sorry, buddy. Still our little fantasy.

My phone buzzes on the counter, making me jump.

It's a fantasy I need to let go of, though, if I'm ever going to fall in love, get married, have kids—all things I want someday.

Flipping my phone screen on, I see a text. *From Kennedy.*

Does she have a sixth sense?

KENNEDY

Any chance you're awake?

I smile and type a reply.

Yep. Couldn't sleep. What are you doing?

I get an immediate text back.

KENNEDY

Standing on your front porch.

Very funny.

I shake my head and set my phone back on the counter, but as soon as I do, there's a knock on the front door.

No fucking way.

Heart pounding, I launch off the stool and run to the front door, unlocking it and throwing it open to see Kennedy's beautiful face.

"Hi," she says, wearing a huge smile.

"Get in here."

I shut the door behind her as she steps inside the house and drops her bags, then I wrap my arms around her in a massive bear hug. God, I've missed her so damn much.

She squeezes me back tightly and sighs softly.

I lean back just enough so I can see her face. "What happened?"

"I got 'laid off.'" She puts air quotes around the words. "Really, the department head hated me and was happy to let me go."

"Ah, Kend. I'm sorry." I hold her close, knowing if she flew here in the middle of the night, it's because she needs me. She needs the comfort of my arms. That's not me being egotistical, I just know her. Kennedy's preferred love language is physical touch. Especially when she's hurting. Knowing how excited she was for this job and feeling like she was finally beginning her career, I know she's hurting a lot right now.

"I missed you," she whispers.

"Missed you more."

She laughs as she loosens her grip and steps back. "Doubt it." Though her eyes are glistening, she has a playful smile on her face, but it softens as she looks around. "Gosh, this place is just the same as I remember it. Still feels like home. Can't believe it's been ten years since I've been back. Definitely not waiting so long next time."

"You better not."

She sighs happily. "Mm. What smells good?"

"Latte and banana bread."

She grabs my arm and her eyes light up. "Gladys's banana bread?"

"Yes, ma'am."

"Gimme."

"Go sit down on the couch. Get comfy. I'll bring it."

She doesn't move, instead staying in place and looking at me reverently. The look is so potent it hits me square in the chest.

"What?" I ask.

She shakes her head. "I really missed you."

I smile and nod toward the living room. "Get settled."

She nods and walks into the living room as I head down the hallway toward the kitchen.

She's really here.

I start her latte, then slice another piece of banana bread and stick it in the toaster oven. My heart's pounding as I glance at the living room.

What if I told her?

I swore to myself a long time ago that I never would, but maybe...

Fuck. What if it ruined everything?

I can't lose her. No one else makes me feel like this. And I guess that's part of the problem. It's not a crush anymore. It's far beyond the desire to fuck her. I love her. My stupid ass is *in love* with her. Maybe I should man up and fucking tell her. Tell her I'm all hers. That I don't want to live without her. That I'm fucking crazy for her, and I'd worship her every single day if she gave me a chance.

Maybe...

Maybe those three sentences would destroy everything.

It's too big a risk if she doesn't feel the same way.

Shaking my head, I finish making her latte, add her banana bread to my plate, and spread some butter on it, then grab my latte and join her in the living room.

She happily takes her mug and pulls her knees up to her chest, nestling into me as I sit in the corner of the oversized leather sofa.

I laugh and look down at her. "What would you have done if I hadn't answered your text?"

Her eyes dance as she looks back at me. "You gave me a key, remember?"

She gave me so much crap when I gave it to her, saying it wouldn't help me, given she was on the other side of the country. But that's not why I gave it to her. I wanted her to know this would always be a safe place for her. Like it is right now.

"I remember you sassing me."

"Well, it was silly. But it would've come in handy tonight. If you hadn't answered, I would've used the key. Then probably would've crawled into your bed and snuggled up to you until you woke up."

Again, physical touch. She's always been snuggly. But does she do that with everyone? What if she could want me? What if she does?

That thought makes my throat dry. Forcing myself to swallow, I look at her.

How the hell do I figure out the answer to this question?

"Kend?"

She stops blowing on her latte and looks up at me. "Hm?"

I stare at her for a moment. Long enough that she raises her eyebrows. Swallowing thickly, I say, "I'm glad you're here."

She smiles and rests her head against my shoulder. "Me too."

Yeah, I'm a chickenshit.

But I can't risk everything on a whim.

I *can* push the line, though. I can test to see what her feelings might be. What she's open to. Whether she might want this too.

If I get even the slightest indication she does...

Well, I'll have to man up.

Until then, it's time to be the most flirtatious, playful version of myself.

Game on.

CHAPTER THREE

Kennedy

I WAKE up to the sound of typing and blink my eyes open. Warmth fills my chest as I look around and realize where I am. I hadn't realized how much this house feels like home, but it does. I'm not sure if it's Devon or the memories here—probably a combination—but it's cozy and comfortable. For the first time in too long, I feel completely at ease.

Realizing I'm lying on a pillow half on Devon's lap, I quickly sit up.

"Morning, sunshine," he says with a laugh. He has a tray table pulled over the edge of the couch and is typing away on his laptop.

"Sorry. How long have I been asleep on you? You must be hungry or need to pee. What time is it?"

He laughs again. "It's nine. You fell asleep about two hours ago. I'm assuming you didn't sleep much on the flight. And have you forgotten what a heavy sleeper you are? I shifted you over, went to the bathroom, then came back and put you on the pillow about forty-five minutes ago."

I rub my eyes and yawn. "Yeah, I'm not someone who sleeps well on planes. Or anywhere remotely public for that matter."

"I know," he says casually. Of course he knows. Most flights I've taken as an adult have been with him. Sometimes I wonder if he knows everything about me. Like he has some kind of direct line to my brain.

"Are you hungry?" I ask as my stomach growls. "Can I make you anything?"

He smiles sweetly at me. "There are bagels in the bread box and eggs and bacon in the fridge if you feel like making some breakfast sandwiches."

"You've missed that, huh?" I ask, remembering how I'd make us breakfast sandwiches every Saturday morning when we lived in New York. He and Justin would come over early with lattes, and I'd make breakfast sandwiches for us, Hallie, and Frannie.

"Constantly. I've made them myself and bought them locally. Even the freshest ones at the farmers' market never taste as good as yours. Must be the love you put in them."

My throat constricts when he says the word love. It's so innocent, and yet there was the slightest inflection to it.

Pushing past it, I say, "Well, as long as you keep things stocked, I'll make them every day I'm here. As long as you make me lattes."

He looks at his computer then back at me. "The best part of running your family business is being able to work from home. And the best part of working from home is taking breaks whenever you want."

Pushing the tray table away, he rises from the couch and follows me to the kitchen.

It's as homey as I remember. Deep maple cabinets and white granite counters with tan and bronze marbling. It's not massive, but its U-shape makes it plenty big enough for us both to move around. The sink sits on one side of the island. The other side is raised for stools to fit underneath. The counter space is plentiful, and as I pull eggs, bacon, and butter from the fridge, Devon turns on the Bluetooth speaker.

I smile at him as I set everything down.

"Music is a must." In college, whenever we'd cook in the tiny kitchenette in the apartment he shared with Justin, we'd always dance around to music.

"Definitely." Then I look around. "Pans?"

He nods, then opens the cabinet by my feet and pulls out a cast iron pan—the best pan for cooking anyone could own. That, a ceramic-coated Dutch oven, a saucepan, and a small pot are all you really need. And when it comes to cooking a breakfast sandwich, there's nothing better than a cast iron pan. Except maybe a full griddle.

"How many slices of bacon do you want?"

"Two's good," he says as *Dandelions* by Ruth B. flows from the speaker.

I open the package and put four pieces of bacon in the pan, then turn it on medium-low. He has a nice gas cooktop which is my favorite for cooking.

"I also have one of these," he says, grabbing a splatter screen from under the cabinet and handing it to me.

"Oh. Nice. Bougie." I pop it on top, then grab the bagels, slice them, and stick them in the toaster oven while he makes our lattes. "You want scrambled eggs or fried?"

"Definitely fried."

With the bacon cooking and the milk frothing, we dance around the kitchen to the song—one of my favorites. Have I mentioned that to him? I know I haven't told him *why* it's one of my favorites. *Because it makes me think of him.*

I close my eyes for a minute, moving to the rhythm of the music when Devon wraps his hand around my waist and pulls me closer. My eyes fly open. And damn it all, my core clenches. Usually I'm past any physical reaction to him. But he's being more physical with me than normal. I'm not complaining, but it's making it harder for me to leave my fantasy world and revert to best friend mode. *I don't want to.*

Especially as he inches closer, his body still moving to the music.

Dance.

I let myself go, having fun. My eyes slip closed again as our bodies move together. Without thinking, I slide my hands under the back of his shirt, running them over his lower back.

His sharp inhale pulls me back to reality, and I rip my hands off his back as my eyes open. I'm expecting to see a freaked-out expression on his face, but instead, he's grinning.

What the hell?

Was he enjoying me dancing so close, rubbing my hands over his skin? My body flushes at the thought, and I turn my attention back to the stove, carefully lifting the splatter screen and using tongs to flip the bacon slices.

"What flavor latte do you want? I have toffee, vanilla, salted caramel, and," he laughs, "chocolate chip cookie dough. I was thinking of you when I bought that one."

I can't bring myself to look at him, but the chocolate chip cookie dough sounds delicious.

"Definitely the cookie dough," I tell him, eyes still on the bacon, as if me staring at it will alleviate the heat coursing through my body or make the bacon cook faster.

He slides the mug over to me, then stands behind me, head dropping down so it's nearly resting on my shoulder.

Oh my god. What's happening?

"Almost done? Should I start the toaster oven?"

Breathe, Kennedy.

One breath in. One breath out.

"Yeah, that would be a good idea."

The bacon is almost done, but really, I need him a step away from me or I might spontaneously burst into flames.

When the bacon is done, I flick off the heat, transfer the strips to a paper towel-lined plate, then turn the heat back on and add the eggs.

"Cheese?" Devon asks.

"American, if you have some."

"Got it."

He puts cheese then bacon on the top halves of our bagels, then butters the bottom halves. When the eggs are done, I put them on the bottoms of the bagels. Then Devon quickly closes the sandwiches and takes our plates to the kitchen counter.

I'm feeling a bit cooler as I sit down next to him, but I'm hoping he keeps his hands to himself. Not because I don't want him to touch me, but because I don't know what him touching me means. I was certain that Devon would never have feelings for me—even if he did, they'd be fleeting. Today, though, I'm not so sure.

"I thought we'd head to the inn after this," he says between bites. "Gladys can't wait to see you."

"I can't wait to see her, either. But what about your parents? Can we stop and see them on the way?"

Sadness flits through his eyes for a moment, but he nods. "Yeah. We can. But... Kend, they aren't going to be how you remember them."

"How bad has it gotten?" I ask. His mom is active on social media and we talk a lot, but she always makes things sound great. Devon hasn't talked much about their health, and since I talk to his mom often, I haven't asked him. It didn't occur to me that she'd be lying about it. But of course she would.

He sighs and spins on his stool so he's facing me. "Dad has to use crutches to get around most days. On good ones, he can use a cane. He had a pretty steep decline last summer, but he's evened out since then. Mom has good days and bad ones, but the ache and weakness in her hips and knees make it hard for her to get out of a chair some days. After having to drop everything several times to go help her get up, because Dad couldn't support her, I finally got them the recliners that can lift you up to standing. I also have aides that check in and help make meals for them. They let me oversee their financials when they sold me the house. I put the money I paid them into an account that I use solely to pay for aides, so I can make sure if they need help, they have it. Luckily, the building has a concierge service if there's an emergency, too."

"Why didn't you tell me?"

He looks at me for a second, then stands up and paces back and forth next to the island.

"Because it kills me. My mom was the one who ran a daycare out of the inn and kept up with every kid. She brought baked goods to every school sporting event I had. She and my dad were involved with everything at the inn. Dad refused to hire a groundskeeper for years because he loved mowing the lawn and taking care of the gardens there. They were active and full of life. I hate seeing what they've been reduced to. When we have kids, they won't be able to play with them. It sucks."

Blowing past the fact that he said "when *we* have kids" because now is not the time to harp on that, I hop off my stool and step in front of him, pulling him into my arms.

"I'm so sorry, Dev."

He melts into my arms, resting his head against mine as he holds me close.

"I'm sorry I didn't tell you."

"It's okay. But I want to support you. I should've come back here sooner."

"No. You were working hard building your career."

"A lot of good that did me," I say with a laugh. He laughs lightly too as we step apart. "I'm here now. And I want to help out. You. Your parents. The inn. Whatever. I'm here for you."

"I know you are." His voice is soft and reverent and his eyes are tender as he looks at me. Again, my body warms and my breath sticks in my throat.

For the briefest of moments, his gaze drops to my lips.

My lips?

No. I'm imagining it, right?

"So," I say, breaking the tension, "let's finish our breakfasts, then we'll go."

"Sounds good," he agrees, sitting back on the stool.

I wait a beat, taking a deep breath and trying to calm my pounding heart and raging hormones because it seems like Devon might *want* me. And I'm not sure what to do with that.

"HEY, where'd you put my stuff?" I call, standing outside the spare room. Maybe he stuck it in the closet in there? All I know is I need to freshen up before we leave the house. Wash my face and put on some clean clothes. Nothing like riding on a plane for six hours to make you feel gross.

Devon steps out of the master, smiling. Or maybe smirking. Or dare I say smoldering?

"I put it in here." He nods toward the master.

Be cool, Kennedy.

"Why?"

"Well, you know Justin is coming."

"Yes." Though he's not a Brighton High alum, he's a close friend to both of us, and since Devon and I are in the same place, he's coming into town for a few days to see us both.

"Rather than have him sleep on that crappy futon, I figured I'd put him in the spare, and you can room with me. You like snuggling at night, anyway." The grin on his face grows, and he gestures for me to follow him into the room.

Taking tiny penguin steps, I follow him, stopping just inside the doorway.

"This dresser," he says, gesturing to one by the window on the far side of the room, "is empty except for the top drawer, so it's all yours. I put your hanging bag in the closet, and if you have any toiletries, you can put them in this bathroom or the hall one, whichever you'd rather use."

"Okay," I choke out. *What is happening?* Devon and I have never even lived together. Not in college or after in New York. Now we're sharing a room? A bed? I'm going to share a freaking bed with my best friend who I have feelings for while trying to pretend everything is normal?

He tilts his head to the side. "Unless, of course, you have a problem sharing a room. Or a bed." Why did that word sound seductive?

Oh my god.

Is he flirting with me?

That grin. Sharing a room. Dancing in the kitchen. He is. He's flirting. Does he want this? Me?

I don't know. And I'm not ready to show my hand until I have a better idea of *what* he wants. But two can play at this game.

Smiling—maybe a little mischievously—I say, "No. No problem. That sounds great." My eyes lock on his and we stare at each other for a moment, heat seeping into the room as we do.

"Perfect," he says. Then he inhales deeply and steps back. "I'll let you get ready."

"Thanks."

He walks out of the room and closes the door behind him.

Holy shit, that was intense.

I have no idea what's going on, but I like it, and I'm going to have some fun with it.

Let's play.

CHAPTER FOUR

Devon

"WAS it weird seeing your old house but not going inside?" I ask Kennedy as we drive up the road to the inn. Instead of stopping at my parents' apartment this morning, we'll be going there for dinner tonight. Mom was set on cooking. Thankfully, her hands and back don't bother her as much as her hips, knees, and feet, so she can still cook—from a chair—and knit, crochet, and do her crossword puzzles. Still, I didn't want her to do too much, so I figured Kennedy and I would show up early to help. Mom would never turn down Kennedy's help in the kitchen. Cooking is something the two often did together.

"Not really. I thought it would be, but something about your house feels more like home. Maybe it's because I spent so much time there, but I think it's partly when I think of my home, I still think of the duplex in Manhattan where I grew up. Where my parents live again now. My house here was a place I lived. Your house was a home. That probably sounds silly."

She tucks a hair behind her ear and looks out the window.

I rest my hand on her thigh and give it a squeeze. "Not at all."

She looks back at me, lips parted in surprise, but only for a second, then she smiles.

I fucking love that my house feels like home to her. I've always wanted her to feel at home there. Maybe now more than ever. When I put her bags in the master, I wasn't sure how she'd react, but I wasn't expecting the playful look in her eyes, the way she stared me down, or that she seems to be playing my game right along with me.

No idea what it means, but I'm taking it as a good sign. She didn't completely shut me down.

A ball of excitement forms in my stomach. *She didn't shut me down at all.*

Out of the corner of my eye, I look at her again.

What if she wants this, too?

I can't get hung up on that thought, but as I pull into the parking lot of the inn, it's the only thing rattling around in my brain.

"SWEET KENNEDY!" Gladys says, standing up from the check-in desk and hurrying over to pull Kennedy into her arms.

"Oh, Gladys, I've missed you."

"I've missed you too, sweetheart. How are you? Devon mentioned your job didn't work out. That is their loss. I'd give your former boss a piece of my mind if I could."

Kennedy laughs and lets Gladys lead her over to the desk. "I appreciate that."

Gladys pulls her reading glasses off her nose, letting them hang from a chain around her neck. She's wearing her typical "uniform" of comfortable pants and a loose floral top. She's got a hippie chic vibe, and she exudes warmth. She's been like a second mother to me, and as my parents' health has declined, I've been even more grateful for her. She keeps the inn running smoothly while also checking in on my parents and trying to take care of me. I don't often let her, mostly because I'm self-sufficient. My mom made sure I knew how to cook, clean, and care for myself by the time I was in high school. She said it wasn't just for my good, it was for hers too, because she wants grandbabies one day and men who take care of themselves are more attractive to women.

Not really sure if that's true since I haven't had a serious girlfriend in over three years. Not that many of the serious ones have been *that* serious, anyway. The last few years, it's been hookups here and there to get me through when my hand wasn't sufficient.

My eyes drift back to Kennedy. What would it feel like to have her sweaty body writhing beneath mine? To hear her scream my name? Watch the ecstasy on her face when she comes? To have her supple pink lips wrapped around my cock?

"Hey," Gladys calls, snapping me out of my haze of lust.

Mostly. Because I've absolutely got a semi now. Thankfully, my cargo shorts shouldn't make that readily visible.

"Huh?"

Kennedy and Gladys snicker.

"Where'd you go? On vacation in your mind? Somewhere warm, I hope," Gladys teases.

Making my way over to the desk, it's impossible to miss the smirk on Kennedy's face. Like she knows where my mind was.

"Something like that," I say, eyes on Kend and drifting down her body. She arches a brow, calling me on it. Then she smiles and turns her attention back to Gladys.

She likes my eyes on her.

I need to find out what else she likes.

"I had some of your banana bread this morning," Kennedy says. "I forgot how good it is."

Gladys chuckles. "Cinnamon is the key."

The door from the kitchen swings open and our longtime cook, Martin, steps out.

"Hey, boss. Glad you're here." He's white as a sheet and looks horrible, though his eyes brighten for a moment. "Kennedy. It's good to see you."

"You too, Martin." She steps toward him, but he holds up his hand.

"You should stay back. Something hit me in the last hour or so. There's no way I can work the rest of my shift. I'll be lucky if I make it home before I—" he gags.

"Get out of here, now," Gladys commands in a firm, motherly voice.

He nods. "Going."

"I'll bring you some soup later, hon," she calls after him.

He waves in response, then staggers out the door and down the stairs.

"Poor Martin," Kennedy says.

"He'll be all right," Gladys says. "But we've got an hour until we open for lunch. Only two reservations today, but several of the guests have been coming down routinely, and you know people from town always stop in. If we're closing, we need to decide."

I glance over at Kennedy. "What do you think? Want to work the kitchen with me? I think the two of us could handle it. It's all sandwiches, salads, soups, and burgers."

She smiles brightly. "I'd love to. Let's do it."

Gladys smiles, too. "Good. Crissy should be in soon to help you out. She had an appointment this morning. All the cold foods should be prepped, it's just a matter of assembly and warming or cooking a few hot dishes."

"After you," I say, gesturing for Kennedy to go first.

We walk through the nearby door that leads down a hallway. Beyond the double doors is the kitchen, gleaming with stainless steel counters and bright white lights.

"Just like I remember," Kennedy says. "When I used to help

Martin in the kitchen some weekends, the first thing he'd have me do was check the pantry."

She turns and walks over to the side of the room where the small pantry is.

Slowly, I follow her, then stand in the doorway, watching her look over the supplies. After a moment, she turns and puts her hand on her hip. "You could help, you know."

"Right. Sorry."

Walking into the room is like walking through a time warp. We could be fourteen looking for something to play spin the bottle with all over again. My eyes follow the same path they did that day, watching her ass stick out as she bends over—though she has a much rounder, sexier ass to look at now—and watching her sweater lift and show off the skin of her low back whenever she presses onto her toes.

She spins around. "You're still not doing anything."

"Do you remember that day?" I ask, lost in the memory.

"Uh, we've known each other a long time, Dev. You might have to narrow it down."

A smile curves up my face. "Spin the bottle."

The words cause her eyes to widen. She sputters for a second. "Yeah. Of course I remember it. Every girl at the party wanted to kiss you." She rolls her eyes.

I step closer. "Yet, when you asked me who I wanted to kiss, I didn't mention their names."

"Devon," she breathes, but I'm not sure if it's out of anticipation or annoyance. So I keep going, resting my hand on her arm, just like I did that day.

"I said there was only one girl I wanted to kiss. Then I grabbed your arm." I run my thumb over her skin. "Just like this. I looked into your eyes. What did you think I was going to do?"

She stares at me for a moment, then licks her lips. They part and my heart hammers. I move closer, still waiting for her answer. Her eyes roll over my face, then she glances at the pantry door, and the magic of the moment is broken. The tension dissipates, and just like she did that day, she steps back.

"It doesn't matter. Because that's when those girls showed up at the door, and I knew..." She takes a breath, looking for the right words. "It would've been stupid."

She doesn't make eye contact with me before spinning around and focusing on the shelves again.

Damn.

All these years, I thought she stopped things because she didn't want more from me. It never occurred to me she was jealous or frustrated by the attention the other girls were giving me.

Wrapping an arm around her waist, I lean down and whisper, "For the record, Kend, it never would've been stupid."

Then I walk out of the room, on fire from those slight touches, and sweating through my shirt.

If we keep going like this, I might combust before anything ever happens with her. But I know with certainty now, I'm not letting her leave Brighton without kissing her, tasting her, letting her know exactly how I feel.

CHAPTER FIVE

Kennedy

DEVON IS MESSING with my head.

And my body.

Maybe my heart.

When he grabbed my arm in the pantry today and looked at me like he did all those years ago, it was almost cruel. Throwing me back into the moment I realized I didn't have a shot with him. But then he wrapped his arm around me, and in one sentence, he told me a truth I'd been afraid to believe in. *It didn't matter that he could have anyone else. He wanted* me.

And God, when his arm was around my waist and his breath was tickling my ear, I'd never been hotter for him. If he'd stayed there for ten seconds longer, I'd have been begging him to close that door, shove my jeans down, and fuck me against the storage racks.

"Kennedy, sweetheart, can you grab some garlic out of the fridge?"

"Sure, Sharon," I say, like I'm not fantasizing about Devon doing dirty things to me while I'm helping his mother cook dinner. I grab a head of garlic out of the fridge and turn back to her. Their apartment has a nice eat-in kitchen, which is perfect for Sharon. She has a rolling office chair so she can get around the kitchen easily, then use the table for all the chopping and prep. "Want me to chop it?" I ask.

She slides me a garlic press and says, "Work smarter, not harder."

I chuckle at that. "I've missed cooking with you."

"I've missed it, too. It's so good to have you home. Though I suppose you see New York as home, don't you?"

"In some ways. I spent my formative years here, though. I think a part of me will always think of Brighton as home."

She smiles brightly at me, then her eyes trail through the kitchen doorway out to the living room where Devon is chatting with his dad. Following her gaze, I watch Devon's arm flex as he brings it to rest on the back of the love seat.

When I look back at Sharon, her smile has grown, but there's something devious in her eyes.

Oh shit.

"Sharon..."

"Honey, if you can look me in the eyes and tell me you don't have even the slightest feelings for my son, I'll let go of this."

"Of what?"

"The hope that one day the two of you will realize what you have is special. And greater than friendship." I stare at her for a moment, opening and closing my mouth several times. She smiles knowingly at my inability to speak. "Good. I'll keep the fantasy alive."

You and me both.

Different fantasies. Same idea, though.

Devon and me.

The thing is, I have no idea if he wants to be with me, if he wants to fuck me, or if he's madly in love with me and wants to marry me tomorrow.

I'm not sure flirting can give me that answer, but that doesn't mean I'm going to stop, either.

AFTER A NICE DINNER with Devon's parents, I'm finally taking a hot shower. Much needed after traveling overnight and all the times Devon made me sweat today purely by his proximity.

It was hard to see how Devon's parents struggled tonight. Sharon tried to pretend she was okay, but every time she stood up, I could see the pain in her eyes. When I chatted with her about it, she said it's just the way things are now, and she has good days and bad days. Devon's dad, Lon, is still the quick-witted man I remember. It's strange to see him struggle to walk or coordinate his movements. Though he didn't show it, his frustration was palpable. I can't imagine mentally feeling like nothing has changed, but to feel my body deteriorating.

Yet, they were both upbeat. Maybe some of it was for my sake, but it seemed genuine. Though it's clear, they're hoping for Devon to get married and have kids soon. Not that they were pushing it, but there were a few side comments. Most of Sharon's seemed more directed at me.

This whole trip has thrown me for a loop. Until this morning, I never considered telling Devon my feelings for him. He's always been the fantasy that would never happen. Now, I'm wondering what *could* happen. More importantly, I'm trying to sort out what I *want* to happen.

The physical attraction is easy, but how do I actually feel for him? Like I want to date him? Do I have a crush on him? Do I... love him? I've never allowed myself to even wonder those things before. Now I'm slowly opening that box, taking my time to figure out what's inside it.

As I rinse my hair and grab the soap, I think back to the physical side of things. How his hand felt around my waist. What it would've felt like for that hand to have slid down my abdomen, inside my jeans, beneath my underwear until his fingers were buried in my pussy and his thumb was swirling over my clit.

I gasp and lean back against the wall, letting myself live out the fantasy with my own fingers, but with my eyes tightly shut, I pretend it's him. His fingers darting in and out of me. The tip of his thumb working my clit. Bracing the wall with one hand, I breathe out heavily, biting my lip.

Oh god. Yes.

No matter how hard I try, I can't hold back my moans.

They get louder until I have to clamp a hand over my mouth, my body jerking and my knees nearly buckling as I come.

Leaning against the shower wall, I slide down, gasping for breath.

"Kennedy?" There's a quick knock at the door. "Are you okay in there?"

Shit. How much of that did he hear?

"Yeah. I'm fine." *Just getting myself off and pretending it was you.* At least I didn't scream his name. "I was just... singing."

Sure, that's believable.

"Okay..."

"I'll be out in a minute."

It's silent for a moment, then he says, "Take your time." His voice is almost sultry, like he has an idea why I need a minute.

What am I doing?

Forcing myself upright, I stand on shaking legs and finish showering.

Once I'm done, I climb out and wrap a towel around my hair and another around my body, then promptly realize... I forgot to grab clothes.

At least I don't have to walk down the hall dripping wet. I

swing open the door, which leads back into the master, and peek out. Seeing the room is empty, I walk over to the dresser, holding the towel in place as I bend over. Not sure where Devon is. Maybe I scared him away with my moans.

Or maybe he went to jack off.

"Kennedy?" Devon's choked voice comes from the other side of the room. I stand and spin around to face him.

Or maybe he went to the kitchen for a glass of water and is now staring at me standing in a skimpy towel.

"Sorry. I was so excited for my shower that I forgot to grab clothes."

"That's fine." But his voice is hoarse and squeaky. Then his eyes trail down my body. For the briefest of moments, I consider dropping the towel. What would he do if I did? Attack me? Take me right here against the dresser?

I'm getting hot all over again.

I need to get out of here.

"I'll be right back."

I skitter back into the bathroom and quickly finish drying off. I run a comb through my hair, planning to let it air dry overnight. I can style it tomorrow. Then I slide on my underwear. I'm reaching for my shirt, when I see one of Devon's Brighton High shirts hanging off the hook on the bathroom door. Smiling to myself, I forgo my tee and shorts and instead slide on his shirt. It's big on me and falls just past my ass.

He had quite a reaction to seeing me in a towel. Time to see how he feels about me wearing his shirt.

I strut out of the bathroom, my other clothes under my arm, and quickly toss them back into the drawer. As I shut it, Devon looks up from his phone. He's shirtless on the bed, and I'm enjoying those defined pecs and abs.

"Is that my shirt?" he croaks.

"Yeah. That okay? It's comfy," I say innocently.

He rises from the bed and moves closer, taking me in. The faintest smirk appears on his lips.

"It's okay. Perfect." His smooth voice sends a chill up my spine.

Realizing the tone of his voice, he steps back and hurries into the bathroom to get ready for bed.

I think I won that round.

A little while later, I'm cozy in bed when there's movement next to me.

"Kend?"

"Hm?" I mumble, flashing my eyes open. Devon lifts my phone from my hand and sets it on the bedside table.

"You need to sleep."

"I think I was."

"I know. Seemed like you were trying to stay up."

I was going to tease him more, but I'm exhausted. Two hours of sleep this morning did not make up for me not sleeping last night.

"I was waiting for you," I whisper, sliding down farther as Devon pulls the covers up. "I like to cuddle, remember? That's part of the point of this, right?"

He looks at me for a beat, then smiles. "Right. Come here." He extends his arm, and I roll over so I'm nestled against him.

For this reason alone, sharing a bedroom was a good idea. I love snuggling with him. After everything that's happened today, I'm still having fun teasing and flirting with him, but I'm also excited to see what happens tomorrow.

CHAPTER SIX

WEDNESDAY

Devon

I WAKE to the sound of quiet breathing, my arm draped over Kennedy's waist and her short brown hair splayed across the pillow next to me. Her arm is resting on mine, and I feel more at home than ever. This is where I'm supposed to be. How I'm supposed to wake up each morning—arms wrapped around the woman I... love.

That's not easy to admit. I feel like an idiot when I do. For spending years with her deep in my heart. At one point last year, I tried to convince myself it was my way of closing off. If I loved her, I didn't have to care for anyone else. Like imagining myself with her was some protective response. So, I spent a few months committed to dating. I know my parents want me to find the right person, get married, and have kids. I want those things, too.

We host speed dating at the inn once a month, so I gave it a go. There was a woman I hit it off with. She was new to the area, and we went out on a few dates, but when it became clear she had feelings for me, I panicked. Not because I didn't want that. God, I wanted that. It would've been so easy had I felt something for her, but I didn't. In the back of my mind, Kennedy was still all I could think about.

I had a few more dates with other women, a couple of whom I also slept with, but I still couldn't get Kennedy out of my head. I couldn't stop imagining myself with her. That was when I had to accept it. It wasn't a crush. Not me trying to avoid a serious relationship. It was Kennedy, my best friend, who, at some point, I'd fallen in love with.

I thought I was completely hopeless until yesterday. From dancing in the kitchen to that moment in the pantry, to last night. God, hearing her moan in the shower about did me in. When I knocked on the door, I mostly did it to make sure I wasn't hearing things. When she awkwardly told me she was singing, I knew for sure.

Damn, I hope while she moaned like that, she thought of me —of all the things I'd do to her perfect body. Then I caught her bent over the dresser in a goddamn towel and I almost blew a load in my pants. I've never run as hot for her as I do right now. Then again, I've never let my feelings for her near the surface before, either. I've been so scared to lose her because of my feelings. I never believed she could have similar ones for me. I still don't know for sure that she does. Maybe she wants to screw me and get it out of her system. Maybe she wants what I do. Maybe she just wants to take a chance and see. I have no idea, but I'm enjoying the fun we're having, playfully pushing boundaries. Like when she walked out here in my T-shirt last night. I saw her take clothes into the bathroom, which means she decided to wear my shirt when she saw it hanging there. Sure, it's comfortable, but I know that's not why she did it.

Now she's lying in my arms wearing a shirt with my last name on it. There's nothing hotter. And my dick has gotten the message. My hard-on is now pressing into her ass, and I'd be worried, but worst case, I can just pretend I'm asleep if she notices.

After a yawn, I pull her closer and close my eyes again, imagining what it would be like to act on my desires. Maybe I'll drift off and dream about it.

Then Kennedy groans and pushes her ass into my rock-hard dick.

My heart stops for a second. Is she awake or asleep? There's no good way for me to find out without getting handsy—which I won't ever do. We're not in a relationship, and I have no idea if she'd be comfortable with me touching her, so beyond where my arm is wrapped around her, I'll keep my hands to myself. Not wanting to ruin the moment, I relax and let this play out.

She groans again and rolls her perfect ass over my cock.

Don't thrust your hips.

She whimpers, and I almost lose it.

Then she lets out a breathy "oh" and I actually think she might be awake.

My dick is painfully hard, and if she presses into it again, I'm worried I'll come. Since I'm only wearing boxers, that would be evident, and I don't want to make this awkward.

Leaning in toward her, I wrap my arm tighter around her waist. "Kennedy?"

She's quiet for a moment, then slowly rolls over, blinking.

"Hi."

"Morning," I say, voice as thick as my cock which is still pressing against her.

She looks down.

Right at it.

Direct eye contact.

"Oh," she says breathily.

"Uh, sorry."

That's right, I'm smooth as fuck.

Her eyes snap back to me, then she bites her fucking lip.

Christ.

"It's fine. Happens, right?" She shrugs one shoulder, but there's an unmistakable glimmer of playfulness in her eyes. Was she rubbing against me on purpose?

I stare at her for a moment, my chest heaving with each breath as I fight the urge to kiss her, own those plush lips.

"If you say so."

Our intense stare down continues for another beat. Then she smiles, tosses the covers off, and climbs out of bed. "I'll get started on breakfast. Feel free to take care of that if you need to."

She gives me a wily smile, then walks out of the room in nothing but my T-shirt and a tiny pair of boy shorts.

I lie back against the bed. Her catching me with a hard-on should've made me feel awkward, but it didn't. Her lighthearted response, continuing to tease me, made me even harder.

I glance at the bedroom door, then down at my cock, but opt not to touch it here. She could walk back in any second. Then I look over at the bathroom. A second later, I'm flying out of bed, across the room, and into the bathroom. Locking the door behind me, I make my way to the shower and turn it on. As steam lifts into the air, I climb inside, water pelting me as I wrap my hand around my hard-as-stone cock.

Kennedy.

I'm shameless as I imagine her on her knees in front of me, lips wrapped around my shaft, my hand twisted in her hair as I fuck her mouth.

I thrust into my fist over and over again, replaying the noises I heard her make last night. Whimpers and moans.

Fuck.

I groan, gasping as I work my hand faster.

She's all I can think about. What does she feel like? Taste like? What does she look like when she comes? I know what she sounds like, and it's on repeat in my head.

Her soft ohs.

My abs constrict as I moan. A shiver runs up my spine and my balls tighten.

"Fuck. Fuck." I run my thumb over my tip as I grunt, squeezing harder, until... "Kennedy." Her name is loud and raspy, rolling off my lips as I come on the shower wall.

Bracing a hand on the wall in front of me, I let the water soak me as my heart pounds in my ears and I struggle to catch my breath.

If it feels that good imagining her, what would it feel like to be with her?

Don't.

There's no time for another hard-on right now.

Getting on with it, I finish my shower, get dressed, and head downstairs.

"Hey," she says, as I walk into the kitchen and plop down on a stool. "Breakfast sandwiches are almost done. Are you... okay?"

Is she asking me if I fucked my hand?

Pretending I don't know what she's talking about, I ask, "Okay?"

"Yeah. I thought I heard you calling for me. I was worried maybe you needed something." She says it with such a straight face, she has to know. She's not that fucking innocent. Especially after what I heard yesterday. She knows.

She turns around and flips the eggs in the pan.

How do I answer that?

Yes. I needed you against the shower wall, water beating down on us as I fucked you from behind.

Then I smile, and I take a page out of her playbook. "No. I was just singing."

She's in the middle of flipping one of the eggs when I say it and she nearly drops it and the spatula. I'm wearing a cocky smile when she spins back to look at me, eyes wide.

"Singing?" she chokes out.

"Yeah. I guess we both like *singing* in the shower."

Her eyes are massive and locked on me.

Still grinning, I hop off the stool, stroll around the counter, and flick the burner off, then croon the titular lines from Brett Young's *In Case You Didn't Know.*

Maybe it's a little heavy-handed, but I do like the song.

She continues gaping at me until the toaster oven beeps. Then she turns her attention to getting the bagels out, buttering them, and assembling the sandwiches.

When she finishes adding the eggs, she turns and shoves a plate in my hand, then says, *"Not Like I'm in Love With You."*

Now I'm staring at her with wide eyes.

She smiles devilishly. "It's a song by Lauren Weintraub. My shower go-to."

She turns and flits past me, plate in hand, and sits down at the island.

Damn, she's good.

"THAT SHOULD BE FINE. I'll be here anyway, so I can—"

"Relax and enjoy yourself," Gladys says sternly. "It's your high school reunion. You *will* enjoy yourself."

I'm sitting next to her at the check-in desk, talking through the details of the reunion next weekend. While our senior class president is in charge of the planning and logistics, since we're holding the reunion here, we have to oversee the details.

Although, apparently, I'm not allowed to help.

"I know it's my reunion, but—"

"No buts. All you are going to worry about is having fun. Especially if it's with a certain sweet brown-haired girl."

Her gaze goes to the dining room where Kennedy is sitting, headphones on and typing away on her laptop.

"I second that," a voice drawls.

Gladys and I both look up to see Justin standing there, bag slung over his shoulder and a smile on his face.

For as long as I've known him, he's looked like a Greek god. Tall, muscular, sandy blond hair, and the kind of smile that melts a woman on the spot. Most women, anyway. A few have been impervious to his charms. Kennedy, for one.

The three of us were inseparable throughout college, and even after, when we all lived in New York together. I'm glad he flew out while Kennedy is in town.

"What are you doing here?" Gladys asks, utterly thrilled. "I thought you weren't coming into town until next week."

His grin grows as he strides over to the desk.

"Dev told me Kennedy came into town early, and since I don't have another modeling job until mid-June, I decided to come early and see my besties."

"Did you really just say besties? I don't think we can be friends anymore."

"It's a valid term. You are one of my *besties.*"

Gladys laughs.

"Don't encourage him," I tell her.

"Hush, you."

"She likes me better," he teases. "It's the accent."

Justin grew up and currently lives in Georgia. Despite going to college in Chicago and then living in New York, he still oozes southern charm, and he knows how to use it. His easy-going attitude and love for attention makes him a perfect model, which was something I recommended he try when he was looking for a job in college. I'd been doing it since high school and had some connections. It was the perfect career path for him, and he makes an excellent living doing it. He found a home in the cover model industry and often appears on romance book covers. A couple of years ago, he parlayed that into audiobook narration, voicing cowboys and southern small-town boys.

"And he spoils me," Gladys says happily as Justin slides her three new books—all with his face on the cover. She flips one open and sees that it's signed by the author. "Signed? You're too good to me, honey."

"Never."

"Suck up," I cough.

"Shut up. Now, where's my girl?"

I openly glare at him, and he laughs so boisterously his belly shakes.

"Aw man, you have it so bad for her. Are you finally going to man up and do something about it?"

Gladys laughs under her breath, and I sigh. I'm not in the mood to explain to either of them that I *am* doing something about it. Even if it's not direct.

"Why don't you worry about yourself?" I nod toward the dining room. "She's in there, but good luck. She's in her own little world."

He chuckles and pulls out his phone, quickly typing out a text and sending it. Then he holds it out to me so I can read it.

Will you get your nose out of your damn computer and come give me a hug?

A second later, there's a smack as Kennedy's headphones land on the table. She flies out of her chair and dashes across the room, leaping into Justin's waiting arms.

Jealousy shouldn't flare in my stomach at their hug. I know nothing would ever happen between them, but damn it, I'm jealous of anyone else touching her.

Fuck, Justin's right. I have to man up and tell her how I feel.

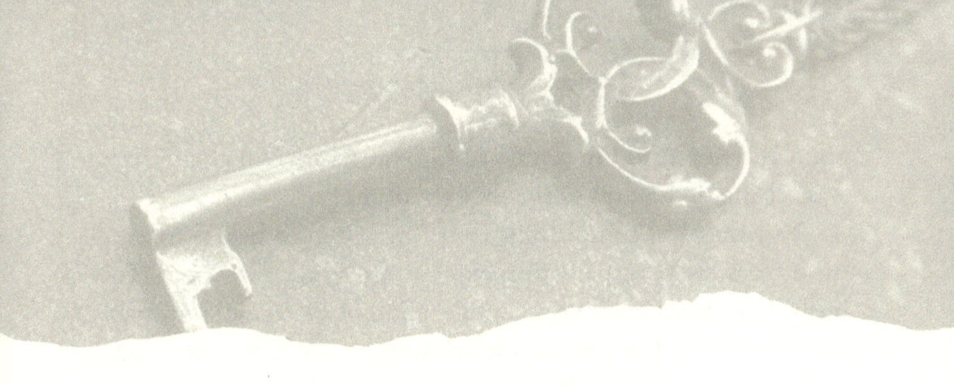

CHAPTER SEVEN

Kennedy

"ANY LUCK?" Gladys asks as I sit down next to her at check-in.

I shrug. "Hard to have luck when I don't even know what I'm looking for. I updated my résumé, but every time I look at a job posting, my stomach turns. I think I need to take a break before I get back at it. My mother told me I should enjoy my time here, and if she is in agreement that I should take a break rather than jump back on the horse, then it's probably a good plan."

"You know we're all happy to have you here. Maybe you should think about sticking around."

"My mother suggested that as well."

My eyes go to Devon, who is laughing with Justin at the edge of the ballroom. They were taping out where things will go for the reunion. I love being here with him, even if I don't quite know what we're doing besides teasing the hell out of each other. When he told me he was *singing* in the shower this morning, I couldn't breathe. The bathroom is directly above the kitchen.

Sound carries. And I'm certain I heard my name. Which means he was getting himself off to the thought of me.

Not that I'm complaining, but I'm still in disbelief. After all these years, we're actually tiptoeing toward a line we've both obviously considered crossing. I feel like an idiot. We should probably talk about it all, but I'm having fun flirting with him, teasing him. Letting him tease me. It's exhilarating, and it keeps me on my toes, never knowing what will happen next.

"Your mother was surprised to find out you're out here."

"Huh?" I say, looking back at Gladys.

She smiles. "Your mom. She didn't realize you'd flown out here."

"Oh. Yeah. I booked the flight on a whim and forgot to tell her until I had to cancel lunch. Wait. How do you know that?"

She pats my hand. "Oh, honey. We have a group chat. Your mother, Sharon, and me. After your family moved back east, Sharon and I made it a point to keep in touch. I always loved your mom. All those nights you and Devon spent camping in the back-yard, we were inside drinking wine, talking, and laughing."

"How did I not know that?"

She shrugs, a mischievous glint in her eye. "You were camping with Devon."

Shaking my head, I elbow her in the ribs. "You're trouble."

"Never. I just know a good thing when I see it." She winks at me. "Now, my dear, unless I'm mistaken, you need to get going if you want to be on time to meet Claire."

My eyes widen as I check the time. "You're right. Today went by so fast. It was nice spending it here."

"Can't say I disagree. I don't suppose I'd have worked here so long if I didn't feel that way."

Leaning down, I kiss her cheek, then grab my bag and head over to the boys.

"I'm headed out. You sure it's okay that I take your car?" I ask Devon.

He fishes his keys out of his pocket and hands me his car key. "Of course. Justin rented a car, so it works out, anyway."

"Okay." I stare at him for a second. A second too long as evidenced by Justin flaring his eyes at me. "Um. I was thinking we should camp in the backyard at some point while I'm here."

A slow smile spreads over Devon's face. "Definitely."

"Sweet. I've heard you two talk about that forever. Can't wait to experience it," Justin says, and we both turn to look at him.

I'm 90 percent sure he's fucking with us, but since I don't know for certain, I say, "Yeah. That would be fun."

"Of course," Devon says, not even trying to fake enthusiasm.

"Anyway, I should go," I say. Then, in a split-second decision, I lean up and kiss Devon on the cheek, something I've never really done before. Hugs? Yes. Snuggling? Sure. Any sort of kissing? Nope. Not even a little cheek peck. Even though this cheek kiss is more than a peck. It lingers until I realize what I'm doing and yank my lips away. My cheeks are burning and his are red too, as Justin watches us like we're a couple of idiots.

We probably are.

"Have fun with Claire," Devon says. "And ask her about karaoke Friday night."

I shake my head. I can't picture Claire doing karaoke, but sure. "Will do. See you at home."

The playfulness slips off Devon's face and his eyes fill with a mix of uncertainty and happiness. It takes me a minute to realize it's because I said home.

"Yeah. Drive safe," he tells me.

I nod and wave as I hurry out of the building.

My mind races as I climb into the driver's seat of his 4Runner and put the key in the ignition.

Am I really thinking of his house as home?

My heart pounds as I hear the answer that both surprises and excites me.

Yes.

CLAIRE DANIELS IS the definition of a boss bitch. She worked her way up at Bloom Beauty and has been the CEO for the last several years. The makeup company has stores all across North America, and is working on breaking into Europe. Claire runs on cigarettes, coffee, and wine and has a general bad bitch attitude that both intimidates and opens doors. Career driven with a fuck-around-and-find-out vibe. We couldn't be more different. Yet, we became fast, if unlikely, friends soon after we met when I first moved to Brighton. She and Devon had been friends since childhood when she went to the small daycare Devon's mom ran out of the inn. They stayed close over the years, and he introduced me.

Maybe it's because our personalities are so opposite that we work. Rather than clash, we balance each other. I keep her in check and she challenges me, never afraid to give me a dose of reality when I need it.

She looks gorgeous as usual as she struts through the wine bar in black sky-high heels and designer clothes. Her long brown hair is perfectly straightened and her makeup is immaculate.

I'm in a pair of tight black jeans, a loose tank, and an unbuttoned flannel shirt with flats. I'm rocking yesterday's curls, a swipe of lip gloss, tinted moisturizer, and barely lined eyes. Normally, I might add mascara to the mix, but I forgot to pack mine.

"Sorry I'm late," she says as she gets to the table where I'm sitting, already sipping on wine. "Some fucker cut me off, and I got stuck at a red light that lasted at least five minutes."

"Good to see you, too."

"Sorry." She slips her coat off and sets her bag down, then smiles at me. "It is good to see you. Especially here. How long are you staying?"

A waiter brings her a glass of wine without asking and she thanks him by name.

"Come here often?"

"At least twice a week. More if I don't have a business meeting involving drinks. I refuse to defile my sacred space with business."

"Makes sense. And as for how long I'm staying... at least until the reunion, if not longer. I'm enjoying taking some time away for once."

"How is it being back in Brighton?"

"Better than I thought it would be."

"And staying with Devon?" She smiles evilly over the rim of her glass.

This is where I would roll my eyes, but things haven't been *typical* between us.

"Interesting," I say honestly.

One perfectly tweezed eyebrow lifts. "Interesting? What does that mean?"

"We've been... flirting a bit."

"Wow. It only took seventeen years to see some progress. Seriously, I don't understand why you've never hooked up with him. Your lady bits need some love. Now you're sharing a house with him—"

"And a bed."

She laughs. "Shut the fuck up. You're sleeping in the same bed and you haven't fucked him? Babe, what are you doing? Why don't you make a move?"

I swirl the wine around in my glass, then glance out the window.

"Because it's not that simple. I don't know what he wants, and if it's not me, that would crush me."

"So instead, you're going to keep giving each other blue balls until you can't think straight anymore? How do you not see how he looks at you?"

I flip my hand through my hair, then meet her fierce gaze. "Maybe I'm starting to."

"Then don't be a dumbass. Take your shot."

We stare at each other for a moment. No one will win this standoff, so I roll my eyes, signaling it's time to move on.

"How's the makeup business?"

"A lot uglier behind the scenes. It's growing, though. London is giving us shit about trying to get a store open there. The number of hoops we have to jump through is ungodly. Business is good here, except Brighton. That fucking store can bite my ass."

"Why don't you close it?"

"Because it's Brighton."

"Aw, look at you being sentimental."

She sips her wine, then looks at me pointedly. "Tell anyone, and I'll kick your ass. You know I can take you."

"Beat my ass is more like it. Yoga and walking are the only forms of exercise I do."

"If you're sticking around, I could use your help."

I choke on my sip of wine. "Mine? I'm not exactly the best person to sell makeup."

"We both know the store sells more than that. And the tinted moisturizer you're wearing, your favorite face wash, and the sunscreen you love all come from there, too. What I need is more help with Brighton than the makeup. One of the girls is out on maternity leave. Any chance you want to fill in? Work your Kennedy magic and talk with the customers? Figure out why they like coming there—or don't. I don't know, but I've got to figure out how to get people in the door."

I shrug. "Sure, why not? When do you need me?"

"Tomorrow?"

"This was a trap, wasn't it?"

She smiles wickedly. "Nope. Just convenient. Nine to two, okay? Call me after and tell me what you learned?"

"What am I? Your spy?"

"If that makes you feel more badass, sure."

"Great."

I take a drink of my wine.

"Hey."

"Hm?"

"I really have missed you, babe."

"Yeah, I've missed you, too."

We tip our wine glasses together and smile.

We may be different as hell, but our friendship is one of the longest lasting I've ever had. We don't get to see each other often anymore, but no matter what, we've always got each other's backs. We don't worry about talking every day because our friendship remains strong regardless. And whenever we're together, it's like no time has passed.

CHAPTER EIGHT

Devon

"SO," Justin says, dropping onto the couch next to me, a beer in hand, "I'm sleeping in the spare room, huh?"

I swallow a swig of my beer. "Yep."

"And Kennedy is sleeping where?"

"My bedroom," I say coolly.

He chuckles. "Well, it's about damn time."

"There's nothing going on. We're just sharing a bed."

At that, he bursts out laughing. "Dude, what's my job?"

"Romance novel enthusiast?" I tease.

"First of all, don't hate. Romance novels are fucking amazing, and that's leaving out the smutty bits. God, I just discovered this new author, and I've been bingeing her series. She has me by the balls. Or the heart. Maybe both. Anyway, to your point, I know romance novels, and let me tell you, you share a bed, sooner or later, you're going to fuck. Now, maybe I'm thinking with my dick, but I can't help but think that's what you want to happen."

"If we're getting into this conversation, I need a full stomach." I reach for the pizza box on the coffee table, but he slams his hand over the top, holding it shut.

"You get pizza when you tell me what's going on here. I've known you for ten years, and you've never come close to making a move. Now, suddenly, you're sleeping in the same bed with her when there's another perfectly good bed available? Is this you finally making a move?"

"Thinking about making a move."

"Jesus, you move slower than molasses on Hoth."

I smack his hand off the pizza box and yank it open, grabbing a slice before he can stop me. "Do girls know you're a closet *Star Wars* nerd?" I ask with my mouth full.

God, one thing I will always miss about New York is the pizza. When Pizza Hut is your best local option, you know society has failed.

"No," he says, grabbing a slice of pizza and leaning back against the couch. "Because that would imply I have actual conversations with the girls I hook up with. But trust me, whenever I meet the right girl, she'll know all about my love of *Star Wars,* and she'll love me for it. Now, back to you and Kennedy. Sleeping in the same bed and you're *kind of* making a move. Why don't you just go for it? What's the worst that could happen?"

"I could lose my best friend?"

He starts laughing so hard at my words that he chokes on his pizza and ends up in a combined coughing and laughing fit.

"Yeah, that's not going to happen."

"How do you know?"

He shakes his head and sets his pizza down. "Let me break it down for you. Remember back in college which of you I became friends with first?"

"Kennedy."

"Yeah. And why do you think that was?"

I shrug. "Because she's relaxed. Fun. Easy to be around."

He makes an obnoxious game show buzzer noise, indicating I'm wrong.

"Nope. It's because she's hot." My eyes fill with fire, and he laughs again. "And that look in your eyes is why I never made a move. I got the sense she had feelings for someone else. Then I met you. Saw how you looked at her, how she looked at you, and decided I didn't want to ruin two possible friendships. Now, don't get me wrong. I don't have feelings for Kend like that. And once I got to know her, any sexual feelings quickly went away since we fell into that sibling-like groove, but it *was* my intention. And if it hadn't been for the way you two looked at each other, I would've gone for it. Basically, the short-and-sweet version is, you've had feelings for each other and been completely blind to it for years, so man up, and do something because she *totally likes you back*," he teases. "Plus, if you don't use it,"—he gestures toward my crotch—"it'll dry up and fall off."

"And if you get a disease, yours will rot off."

Justin shakes his head and takes another bite of his pizza. "Change the subject all you want, but stop acting like I'm not right, because I am. You two want each other. One of you just has to find your nads and go for it."

I grimace as I take another bite of my pizza.

I can't believe he only became friends with Kennedy because he wanted to hit on her.

Sure, let me pretend that's why I'm annoyed.

It couldn't possibly be anything else he said, or that he's so fucking right it hurts.

I'm a chicken shit.

KENNEDY'S soft footsteps across the floor wake me from sleep. In the dark, I see her moving across the room to the dresser. She opens the bottom drawer, then pulls something out. Closing it again, she stands up, then shimmies out of her tight jeans. I watch the curve of her ass in the moonlight. Her soft, supple skin that I ache to run my hands over. Then she takes off her flannel shirt and drops it on the floor before lifting her tank over her head and undoing the clasp of her bra.

I slam my eyes shut. I have no idea if she knows I'm awake and she's teasing me, but my mother raised me right, so no matter what I might want to see, I'm not going to without Kennedy's express consent. I saw her ass yesterday and this morning, not to mention for many years in swimsuits, so I felt okay about that.

The bed shifts and I slowly open my eyes again. "Hi. What time is it?"

"Almost one." She settles under the covers and lies on her side, facing me. "Sorry if I woke you. I was planning to be back earlier, but I didn't want to drive while buzzed, and a glass of wine turned into half a bottle. You know Claire."

"Sounds about right."

"I texted you, but since you didn't answer, I figured you were asleep."

"I'm glad you were safe."

My gaze lingers on hers. Then, without thought, my eyes drift down to her lips.

"Devon," she breathes, and my eyes dart back to hers. She runs a hand through my hair and looks deep into my eyes. Then she yawns big and sighs. "I'm tired."

"Yeah, me too," I say, even though I've never felt more awake.

I roll onto my back and extend my arm. She hesitates for a moment, then rolls over, resting her head on my chest and draping her arm over my stomach.

She's silent for a few moments, and I assume she's asleep, but then she says, "I like this. Snuggling with you."

"So do I," I whisper back, heart pounding.

I pull her closer, and her body grows heavy against mine.

Well, there's always tomorrow.
Assuming I find my balls before then.

CHAPTER NINE

THURSDAY

Kennedy

"HEY, YOU BUSY NOW?" I ask Claire over the phone as I sit in Devon's car outside the local coffee shop, Busta Brew, blowing on my latte.

"No, I'm just driving. How was the store today?"

"It was good. Better than I thought it would be, honestly. I think I've figured out a couple of your issues."

"Hit me."

"First, people seem unaware that it's there—or what it is. One person said they hadn't realized until recently there was one in Brighton and they were going to one in San Fran. Another didn't realize what the store was, and it was her first time visiting. She'd been shopping at the place next door and decided to stop in. She was thrilled to find so many makeup and skin care products locally and loved that you offered free samples. She left with a huge bag of stuff. I think getting word out about what your business is and that it's there in Brighton are the most essential things. And typical stuff won't work here—online ads or whatever else. People here rely on word of mouth for so much. Which got me thinking. You definitely have a market here, so what if we hosted an event to get people in the door?"

"What kind of event?" she asks, her voice echoey.

"I'm thinking some kind of girls' night in. We could have wine, facials, maybe even makeup tutorials. If we mention it at some of the local businesses or even offer to let them have some products there, word of mouth will spread. Also—and I can't believe Devon or Gladys never thought of this—you should have your skincare products at the inn. People love free samples and knowing they could get more right in Brighton if they love them would be huge. Devon said they're booking more and more weddings there, so you could even negotiate something to have some products in welcome baskets or favors."

"Jesus, Kend. You sure you didn't major in marketing? I have an entire team for that, and none of them have suggested it."

"Because they're good at marketing. What you need is someone good at Brighton. Or the people here, at least."

"And that's you. You fit there. Always have. Unlike me."

"I don't know about that."

"It's true. Speaking of, did you make a move on Devon last night?"

"No," I say nonchalantly. "It was late."

"And guys are never horny late at night. Grow some ovaries. Honestly, I'm getting blue balls for you. This is ridiculous. Your hooha was meant to be used and abused, babe. You're treating it like a fancy restaurant you have to have reservations for."

"And you treat yours like a McDonalds. That's not my fault. It's quality over quantity."

"Rude. It's not a McDonalds. It's a Burger King, if anything. You can have it your way." She laughs, the sound reverberating around her car and echoing through my phone. "And by the way, if you think Devon wouldn't be a *quality* lay, you're kidding yourself."

"I'm sure it would be... fucking amazing, okay? But I'm not *having him my way* until I know how he wants me."

"You know a good way to find that out?"

I sigh dramatically. "I'm sure this is going to involve me getting naked."

"It wouldn't hurt, Kend. That's all I'm saying."

"Well, thanks for the advice."

"Happy to help. And thanks for your advice. I'll think it through and come up with a plan. Talk later."

"Yeah. Oh, hey, any chance you want to join us for karaoke tomorrow night?"

She makes a weird wheezy sound, and it takes me a minute to realize she's trying not to laugh. Finally, she can't hold it back anymore and bursts out laughing.

"Karaoke? No fucking way. I'd rather stick something sharp in my ear than go to karaoke. Actually, same effect."

"I told Devon he was crazy to think you'd come, but he thought you might get enjoyment out of watching drunk people make idiots of themselves."

"Even that is not worth bleeding from the ears."

"Noted."

"Okay, I gotta go, babe. Talk to you later."

"Bye."

She hangs up, and after a sip of my latte, I pull out of the parking lot and head for the inn.

"WHAT DO YOU THINK?" I ask Devon and Gladys after I've told them about my idea to have some of Claire's skin care products at the inn.

"It's smart," Gladys says. "And I'll be sure to add her to the list of shops we recommend people check out. Since it's not right downtown, I didn't have it on there before."

"I agree. It's a good idea. And we can mention it to any brides who come through. Maybe if Claire has someone on staff who does makeup, we could recommend them as a wedding day option. At the very least, we could offer a discount to brides who purchase through Bloom Beauty."

"Oh, I hadn't thought of that, but that's perfect. And if the bride and bridesmaids wear the products and like them, we can direct them to Bloom. If they're local, they can buy more at the Brighton store, and if not, it's still new customers for her."

"Well, maybe you should forget about writing and go into marketing," Gladys says.

"I don't know about that," I say with a laugh. "Social media is the bane of my existence. I only use it for book groups and keeping up with my family. But I'm a good people person, and I think that's what she needs."

"Working here at the inn, helping Claire. Before you know it, you're going to be like Kirk from *Gilmore Girls* with all the jobs in town," Gladys says with a grin.

"It's just temporary," I say with a laugh, causing Devon's eyes to darken. "At some point, I'll need an actual job." Even if what I've been doing here is a lot more fun.

I'M GETTING comfortable in bed when Devon walks into the room shirtless, in gray mother effing sweats. Why are they sexier than other colors? Seriously, I was shopping for sweatpants the other day and saw some unisex ones. I flicked through all the colors and stopped to ogle the male model in the gray ones only. Exact same picture and I couldn't see any peen outlines, but still, the gray was sexier.

At this point, he might know how women feel about a man in gray sweats and he's doing this on purpose. Every day our teasing reaches a new level. I'm not complaining. It's fun seeing how he'll react and getting that little thrill every time he says or does something I'm not expecting.

"You okay?" he asks, and I realize I'm ogling him like I did the sweatpants model.

"Fine. Just thinking you should be a sweatpants model."

He stops in his tracks and looks down. Then he grins. "Oh? Why? Do they look good on me?"

Why bother pretending? Claire made a good point that I won't know if I don't try. I might not be as brazen as her, but I can keep having fun with this. Eventually, there will be a moment, right? Or one of us will break. Maybe we'll both break at the same time in a super-hot moment where we rip each other's clothes off, and then—oh god. Claire's right. I do need to get laid.

"Kennedy," Devon rumbles, sitting down on the edge of the bed next to me, his eyes burning into me. If I wasn't horny before...

"Hm?"

"I asked if you thought I look good in these. Then you spaced out." He raises his eyebrows.

Clearing my throat, I lean forward and run my hand along his waistband. "You look hot in these." His eyes widen as I lean closer, and he swallows hard. "So hot you should probably take them off." Then I pull on the waistband and snap it against his stomach before leaning back as I laugh.

"Oh, you think you're funny?"

He stands up as I continue laughing. Then, the smile slides right off my face as he pulls the waistband away and rolls his hips while slowly pulling them down, leaving him in tight boxer briefs.

Don't look at his penis. Don't. Do not. No peen.

I force my eyes up to the ceiling, and now he's laughing. He drops the pants on the floor and climbs onto the bed, purposely climbing over me to get to his side. "Now who's hot?"

I smack his chest as he sits down beside me.

"Hey, Dev?"

"Yeah?"

"Have you ever thought about modeling again?"

He tosses the covers up and slides underneath them, flipping his lamp off as he does, so mine is the only one illuminating the room.

"I still model sometimes."

"For charity and local stuff, but I mean get back into it. Maybe not what Justin does, but..."

"Honestly? Not really. Sometimes I think about it. There were parts of it that were fun for sure. When Justin and I did that underwear campaign in our early twenties, we had so much fun. But as social media became a fixture in everyone's lives, it just got harder for me to enjoy it. I'm not like Justin. I don't want to take pictures with fans at every Starbucks I walk into. Why do you ask?"

I shrug. "Just curious what you see for your future."

"Oh. This... I guess."

"Sound more excited," I tease.

"It's not that I'm not excited. I guess I just feel like I'm already living my future. Or rather, that what comes next isn't about a job."

"That makes sense."

"What about you? What does your future look like?"

I groan. "You weren't supposed to ask me. I barely know what next week looks like, other than the reunion."

"Okay, what would the dream be?"

I shrug. "I don't know. Thus far, it's always been to build a career at a long-lasting online magazine or news site, and hopefully writing more meaningful pieces as I go. Right now though... I don't know. Maybe I'm chasing the wrong dream."

"Or maybe you're burned out and need a break. Have you considered leaving New York? Trying to find a job in a different city?"

I nod slowly. "A little." *I've been considering it a lot more these last few days.* "Right now, I'm trying to figure out what I want most of all, then I'll figure out where. Until then, I'm enjoying being here. With you."

He searches my face for a moment, then smiles softly. "I'm enjoying it, too."

Flipping my light off, I slide under the covers. My stomach ablaze, I snuggle against him, curling my body around his.

I have no idea what we're doing anymore. It's terrifying, but I like it.

"Hey, what are you thinking about for your future if it's not your career?"

"Oh. Um, personal stuff, I guess. Falling in love, having kids."

I lift my head to look at him, only to find him staring back at me. Desire wraps around me as heat fills the space between my legs. I could kiss him right now, but at that thought, I can't breathe. My chest tightens, and I'm not sure if it's out of fear or excitement.

"Anyway," he continues, "that's further down the line. Like you said, I'm just enjoying where I am right now."

His lips graze my forehead, and he pulls me closer. As I rest my head on his shoulder again, he gently strokes his fingers down my arm, over and over, as my eyes grow heavy and I slowly drift off to sleep.

CHAPTER TEN

FRIDAY

Kennedy

TODAY IS A *ME* DAY. It's been way too long since I had one, and it feels so damn good. I started my day with breakfast at the inn. Now I'm headed to the local library.

Libraries are one of my favorite places to visit. The one in Brighton isn't massive, but it has a surprisingly large and eclectic selection. It seems like the type of library that stocks what their residents ask for more than whatever is "typical." That's my kind of library because it means they'll be more likely to get a book for me if I want it. I can't believe I'm even thinking that, but... I've been growing more attached to Brighton. I'm not sure what my next career steps are, but I've been thinking I'll take a little extra time to decide that. If Devon is up for having me, I'd love to stay here for the entire summer.

As I bring my small pile of books to the checkout desk, I see a sign that reads "Volunteers Needed."

"Hi, there. All set?" A woman with graying dirty blonde hair tucked in a bun walks over to me. She looks to be about Gladys's age.

"Yes. Hi, um, I believe Gladys called. I'm a friend from out of town and she was going to let me use her library card to feed my reading addiction."

The woman nods. "Yes. I thought you looked familiar. Kennedy, right? Leann's girl?"

I chuckle at that. "Yep. That's me. Between being around town and helping out at the inn, it's been a test of my memory—I remember some faces, but rarely names."

She takes the pile of books and the library card from my hand and begins scanning them.

"Well, I'm Cindy. I run this little slice of heaven. Let me know if you need anything."

I tap the sign. "Looks like you're the ones who need help. What kind of volunteer help do you need?"

She smiles brightly as she slides the books back to me. "Oh, mostly shelving books, assisting people with finding books, and running book clubs. Any of that sound good to you?"

"All of it?" I smile too. "I love books. Always have. And I'm good at hooking people up with the right books. If I don't know about it, I know where to look to learn more. I'm not sure I've ever been to a book club, but I'm up for helping however I can. Do you have a romance one? I read most genres, but I read romance the most, especially indies."

Cindy clasps her hands together. "Yes. Actually, that's our most popular one. It's on Tuesdays. If you're willing to come and maybe help guide the conversation about it, that'd be great. If you think you have time to read the book."

"Which is it?"

She gives me the name of the book, and I laugh to myself. I read it a month or two ago with Hallie and Frannie. And guess who is on the cover *and* narrates the audiobook?

"I've actually read it already. Has Gladys ever come to the book club?"

Cindy laughs. "Oh, no. She says reading is her solo activity and discussing the books makes her feel like she's back in high school. Why do you ask?"

"Oh... I just know she's read that book. Because we know the cover model slash narrator of it."

"You know Justin Ayers?" another woman screeches. She appears from behind some shelves at the back of the desk. "Gladys knows him?" She smacks Cindy's arm. "She's been holding out on us!"

"You said the next book club is this Tuesday, right?"

"Yes," Cindy says.

"How would you like to meet him? He's in town right now," I say.

The other woman screeches again.

I stifle a laugh and look at Cindy. "How come she's not leading the book club?"

"Oh, I help, but I have a tendency to get a little *passionate*. I find it's best if I'm not in charge. I'm Lily."

"Lily, nice to meet you. I'm Kennedy. So, what do you think?"

Cindy is in a slight state of shock. "If you can convince him, we'd love to have him."

"He's one of my best friends. I'll make it happen."

"Oh my gosh! I'm so excited," Lily squeals. "Gosh, he's so hot. Like *hot*. There's this campaign he did with another guy. They were both modeling underwear. It was years ago..."

I'm laughing now.

"Sorry. Uh, that other guy is my best friend, Devon. He runs the inn."

Her eyes widen and her cheeks go pink. "Oh my god. Really? How did I not know this? And oh gosh, I've totally gushed about him to my husband and my husband probably knows him. I'm *mortified.*"

This girl is my kind of crazy. She reminds me a little of Frannie.

"Are you not from around here?"

She shakes her head. "Grew up in San Diego. My husband is from San Francisco, but he got a job here at the local hospital."

"Oh, cool."

"I'm mostly a stay-at-home mom and avid reader, but now that both of my kids are in school full time, I work here part time during the day. And book club is my *me time.*"

"Well, I'll try to make it worth your while this week," I tell her.

"Thank you so much," Cindy says.

I fish a card out of my bag that has my name and contact info on it.

"Give me a call or a text and let me know when you need volunteers the most. I'd love to help out with that as well. And I'll talk to Justin tonight and get it all set up."

"Thanks, dear. Glad to have you here."

Lily grabs a piece of paper and scribbles something down before sliding it to me. "This is me shooting my shot. I haven't made many friends here, but you seem nice, so if you want to grab coffee or anything, I'd love that."

"That sounds great," I say, slipping the number in my bag. "I'll text you."

She does a little happy dance. "Okay. Have a good day!"

"Thanks, you two as well. Take care."

I wave as I turn and walk toward the door.

I got some great books, a fun volunteer gig, and a new friend out of this.

When was the last time I made a new friend randomly like that? Hardy and Ackley were a package deal with Mark when Frannie started dating him. But other than that, I can't remember the last time I easily connected with people. Of course, most people in Manhattan aren't interested in a friendly chat and giving some random girl at the library their number so they can be friends. Maybe that's why.

That's it. Decision made. I'm staying all summer.

AFTER THE LIBRARY, I went to Busta Brew and got a latte. It was almost as good as the ones Devon makes, which is a high compliment. Then I stopped back home and dropped off my books before going for a short hike on a nature trail. Justin was nice enough to let me borrow his rental car today, since he was spending the day at the inn with Devon. I topped off my day with a nice long shower—no *singing* this time, which is good because Devon and Justin got home halfway through. Then I took time to put on lotion and blow dry my hair.

Feeling relaxed and a little sexy, I stroll downstairs.

"How much do you love me?" I ask Justin as I walk into the kitchen.

Justin's eyebrows go up and he looks from me, then across the kitchen to Devon, and back again. "Who are you asking?"

The slightest bit of pink hits my cheeks, but I push the feeling away.

"You. I need a favor."

Justin grins. "Hit me with it."

"How would you feel about making an appearance at the library next week?"

His smile grows. "What kind of appearance?"

"A romance cover model slash narrator appearance at their romance book club. I mean. Don't dress like a cover model. Leave your shirt on. Don't give them horny eyes."

Devon snickers from the corner. "Horny eyes?"

I turn toward him. "Yeah. Horny eyes. Have you never seen one of his covers? Where his eyes simultaneously scream *I'm the guy who will worship you* and *I can't stop thinking about how I want to fuck you tonight.*"

Devon's eyebrows go up and he turns to Justin, who is still grinning.

"That's exactly it. I never put words to it before. It's more of a feeling," Justin says.

"So, will you do it? It's on Tuesday." I tell him which book they're reading. "Maybe you could sign some books and do a little reading? Take some pictures?"

"Sure. Why not? Sounds fun."

"What inspired this?" Devon asks, amused.

I explain about volunteering and how Cindy and Lily reacted to finding out I know Justin. For Lily's sake, I leave out the part about her knowing who Devon is. Then I tell them how I offered Justin up as a sacrifice.

Justin chuckles. "Sounds like a fun night. Just tell those ladies not to get too handsy." He winks at me.

"I will be sure they know that. Oh, and if you have any indie authors you've worked with who you think would be good to feature for future book clubs, let me know."

"Will do," he drawls. Then he smiles.

"What?"

"You seem happier here. It's good to see." Then he rises from his stool and walks past me out of the room, ruffling my hair as he goes.

Devon strolls over as I digest Justin's comment.

He said *happier*, not happy. Happier. Implying I wasn't as happy back in New York. Or anywhere else he's seen me. Is that true? Am I happier here? I'm having fun. I feel free in a way I never have before. And then there's the man standing in front of me.

"You do look happier here," Devon rumbles.

My gaze snaps to his, to his deep green eyes. Eyes that now exude the same look I described a few minutes ago.

"I do?"

"Mhm." He steps closer and wraps an arm around my waist. "It's like you belong here."

"Devon," my voice cracks.

"Hm?"

"I—I..." *I what? What the hell am I even saying?* His proximity has me so hot I can barely think. "You're—why are you looking at me like that?"

"Like what?"

"Like you want to fuck me on the counter." *Oh god. Why did I say that? Of all the things I could have said, why* that?

He smirks, leaning in closer. "Is that what you want?" My eyes widen and my heart flies to my throat. I can't answer. I don't even make a noise. All I hear is the sound of my own breathing. His grip on my waist tightens, then he kisses my head and steps back, but not before whispering in my ear, "Because I do."

Holy shit.

And as he walks down the hall away from me, he says, "I'm going to take a shower. Just in case you hear me *singing.*"

I can't breathe.

I stand, frozen in place, staring at the wall of the kitchen until a door closes upstairs and I hear the water turn on. Then I dash up the stairs, sneak into the bedroom, grab my iPad, and run across the hall to the office, locking the door behind me.

I fire off a text to Frannie and Hallie.

> About to video call you both. This is a 911 call, so you better answer!

A moment later, my iPad is set up, and Frannie and Hallie appear on my screen as they answer my desperate plea for help.

"What's the emergency? I'm assuming it's not a real one since we're an entire country away," Frannie says.

Hallie leans in toward the camera. "No. This is definitely Devon related. See the mix of panic and lust in her eyes?"

"Ah," Frannie nods in agreement. "Well, don't keep us waiting! Tell us."

"I think Devon wants me."

False. I know he wants me.

"Wow," Frannie says, at the same time Hallie says, "Oh my god." Except, both their voices are flat.

"What was that?"

Frannie stares at the camera. "Me or you, Hal?"

"Oh me, please," Hallie says. "This is fun."

"What's fun?" My hands are shaking. There's nothing *fun* about this.

"You being surprised that Devon has a thing for you."

"I said he *could.*"

"Well, he absolutely *does,*" Frannie says.

Hallie nods in agreement. "But based on the look on your face right now, I think we need some background."

Without a second thought, everything rushes out of me. How things felt different, teasing each other, the tension surrounding us every second, and what just happened in the kitchen.

"Damn," Frannie says.

"It's about time," Hallie agrees.

"About time for what?"

"For you two to stop ignoring how great you could be together," Frannie says matter-of-factly.

Swallowing hard, I stare at the screen, completely overwhelmed.

"What's wrong?" Hallie asks.

"What if... he doesn't *want* me? What if he thinks it would be fun to hookup? Or mess around while I'm here? I couldn't do that. Or..." I trail off, my biggest fear hitting hard and leaving me on the verge of tears. "What if he does want more—everything— but we ruin it? This is why I never wanted to consider doing anything with him."

"Okay, I think we need backup," Frannie says.

"Agreed."

"Backup? What do you mean?"

Hallie taps away at her screen, and a moment later, there's a request for Ryan Hardison to join the call. And then Brian Ackley. I let them both in at the same time Mark appears next to Frannie.

"What's up, baby girl?" Ryan asks. "Shit, why do you look sad? Do I need to fly out there and kick someone's ass?"

"I'm coming, too," Brian says.

"She's worried about how Devon feels about her since they've been sharing a bed—"

"And he told her he wants to screw her on the kitchen counter!" Hallie shouts, cutting Frannie off.

"Sounds to me like it's clear what he wants," Mark says.

"She's scared of what would happen if they crossed that line," Frannie clarifies.

"You said he's being sweet to you," Brian says softly. "What do you mean?"

"We're sleeping in the same bed, cuddling at night. Last night when we were snuggling in bed, he asked me what I wanted out of the future. I asked him too. It seemed like we were both talking about each other, but—"

Then Hardy cuts through the bullshit. "Baby girl, are you in love with him?"

I'm silent for a moment as they all stare at me. A screen full of eyes boring into me.

"I've tried really hard never to ask myself that question," I finally admit.

"I think you need to now," Hallie says. "You need to know what you want, so you know how to deal with this."

"Agreed," Frannie says.

"Okay. Maybe. What do I do in the meantime?"

"You could talk to him?" Mark offers.

"Or, if you're too chicken to do that, you could always turn that flirting back to something sweet until you work up the courage," Brian says.

I nod slowly.

"Don't let fear hold you back. Have fun. Be honest with yourself. Then with him," Hardy says.

"How do you know so much about all this?" I ask him.

"Those who can't do..." Brian teases.

"Shut up. Everything in life is easier when you're not in the middle of it. Think of how easy it was to be objective about Markie Mark and Frannie. Obviously, they were meant to find each other, but they were both acting like scaredy cats."

"Thank you for that," Mark deadpans.

The fan in the bathroom switches off, and I know my time is up. "I've gotta go. This actually helped. Thanks. Love you guys."

There's a chorus of "love yous" and "goodbyes" as I end the call.

Then I stare at the blank screen of my iPad. *Do I love him?*

I still don't want to answer that question. But I know I can't keep pushing these boundaries without knowing for sure what he wants, which means after karaoke tonight, I need to finally talk to him. All this flirting is fun, but I need to know where it's going. It's scary as hell, but it's time to address the massive elephant in the room.

Once I hear Devon go downstairs, I walk back to the bedroom and grab my outfit for tonight—black jeggings and a maroon V-neck tank with a light gray cardigan. Then, I head to the bathroom to wash my face, put on my barely there version of makeup, and tousle my short brown curls. I miss my long hair and still hate myself for cutting it for that jackass boss of mine.

That feels like a million years ago now. Maybe Justin's right. Maybe I am happier here than I realized.

With one last look in the mirror, I walk downstairs and find Devon standing alone in the kitchen, lost in thought.

Walking over to the far side of the kitchen, I grab a glass out of the cabinet and get some water from the fridge. Devon still hasn't said anything by the time I've finished drinking it.

"You okay?"

His eyes lift and he looks at me for a moment like he's just realized I'm here.

"Yeah. Sorry. Just thinking."

My eyes inadvertently go to the counter. "About, um"—I clear my throat—"what you said earlier?"

A smirk plays on his lips, but he shakes his head. "No. I was thinking about what it would be like to have you here every day. If you stayed."

My heart leaps. "You want me to stay?" Reaching for him, I step closer, resting my hand on his arm.

"I want you to be happy. Selfishly, I hope that's here." He tucks some of my hair behind my ear, looking at me intensely.

"Devon," I breathe as his eyes drop to my lips.

Fingers pressing into his arm, I inch toward him as he does the same until our chests are almost touching.

Our eyes meet again, tension swirling around us, growing thicker by the second.

My breaths grow heavy and my heart beats faster as I look into his eyes, finding a mixture of intensity and vulnerability.

Slowly, he dips his head down as I lift onto my toes.

I'm lost in the moment. All I hear are the sounds of our breaths and my heart pounding in my ears as our lips move closer and closer. So close I can feel his breath on my face.

"Hey! Y'all coming?" Justin calls from the front room.

I jerk my head back and we both step apart, still trying to catch our breaths. The moment is broken, but the tension is not.

Letting him know I liked where that was going, I lean up and kiss his cheek, then squeeze his arm before moving past him out of the room.

My heart's still beating erratically as I grab my purse and the three of us walk out to the car. He wants to fuck me on the kitchen counter, but he also wants me in that kitchen every morning. I don't know what this means for us, but I know I want to find out. I need to.

When we get back from karaoke, I intend to pick up where we left off. Preferably in the bedroom.

CHAPTER ELEVEN

Devon

"SO, are you going to tell me what happened between you and Kennedy?" Justin asks in a hushed voice as we walk away from Kennedy—who grabbed a free table—to get drinks at the bar.

"What do you mean?" I ask like I haven't been acting weird as fuck from the moment we left the house. He grabs my arm, stopping me in my tracks, and simply raises his eyebrows at me. "Yeah. Okay." I nod toward the bar. We order drinks for ourselves and Kennedy, then I look at Justin, who is giddy with excitement. "We almost kissed."

His eyes widen and a grin breaks out. "No shit?"

I rub the back of my neck. "No shit."

"What stopped you? And why do you look like you got hit by a train?"

My eyes drift over his shoulder to where Kennedy is bouncing in her seat to the upbeat Taylor Swift song playing.

"Because I'm acting like a fucking moron. Earlier I told her I

83

wanted to fuck her on the kitchen counter. We've been flirting and teasing each other and alluding to sexual things, but then I barreled over the line and she looked terrified. Maybe a little turned on, but mostly horrified. Then I implied I was going to jack off to her in the shower." I huff and run a hand through my hair.

"You're a fuckin' mess. Where does the kissing come in? Oh, did she join you in the shower?"

"What? No. Fuck, you've been narrating too many romance novels. When I finished my shower, I went downstairs, and I was replaying what I said to her and panicking. What if I scared her away? That's the last thing I'd want. I realized how badly I want her to stay. Not just for a few weeks or the summer, but forever. I want her here with me. Then she walked into the room and asked me what I was thinking about—alluding to what I said about fucking her on the counter. I didn't want her to think that's all I wanted, so I told her the truth. It was a perfect moment. We were this close"—I hold my thumb and pointer up, pinched close together—"to kissing. Then you yelled from the other room. So, thanks for ruining that."

He laughs as the bartender sets our drinks down.

"Well, you know what you have to do now, right?"

I stare blankly at him. *Tell her how I feel? Kiss the hell out of her? Beg her to stay? Fuck her on the kitchen counter?*

Then he nods toward the stage and grins.

Ah, fuck.

NORMALLY KARAOKE IS fun and ridiculous. If I have enough to drink, I might get up and do a goofy rendition of an '80s song. Otherwise, I sit and enjoy the desecration of some of my favorite songs. Never have I come to karaoke and purposely performed well. Until tonight.

Why did I let Justin talk me into this? It's his fucking accent. It makes everything sound like a good idea.

Now I'm walking onto a crappy stage where all eyes are on me, but I look for the only eyes that matter.

Kennedy's are wide, but there's a smile on her face. Of course, she doesn't know what I'm about to do. My stomach churns as the opening bars of *One of Them Girls* by Lee Brice play. This is a ridiculous plan, but it's too late to take it back, so I look at Kennedy, open my mouth, and commit to this.

I picked this damn song because it's always made me think of Kennedy. For the most part, she doesn't give a fuck about what other people think. Guys look at her like she's candy, and somehow, she doesn't notice. She's the girl I'd give everything to have, and she doesn't realize it.

As the chorus begins, I lose myself in the words. Words that tell her exactly what I want. *Her.* That I'd do anything to have her.

Her gaze on me is intense and hard to read, but she can't take her eyes off me, and that fuels me. Pulling the mic from the stand, I move around the small stage, the song flowing out of me. Most people don't know I can sing well. Kennedy is one of the few. When we'd camp in the backyard, she'd always force me to sing to her while we roasted marshmallows. Of course, there wasn't much forcing needed. I'd do anything for her. If it makes her smile, I'll do it without a second thought.

People are clapping and singing along with the song, but my eyes are still on Kennedy as she watches me raptly, her face impossible to read. I want to believe I see some excitement in those eyes, but it's hard to know from here. And singing right in front of her might be a touch dramatic. Instead, I place the mic back in the stand, holding onto it as I sing the final words, still watching her. Emotion clouds her face, and I'm not sure that's a good sign or a bad one.

The second the song is over, I hop off the stage, but a couple of people step into my path and compliment me.

I politely thank them while trying to get away quickly. When I finally get to where Justin and Kennedy were sitting, they're standing and seem to be arguing.

"No, it wasn't!" Kennedy yells, then bolts out of the bar.

"What the hell was that?" I ask Justin.

He scrunches his face and says, "It's possible this wasn't as good of an idea as I thought."

"Where did she go?" I yell. He opens his mouth but doesn't say anything. "Justin!"

He glances over his shoulder, then turns back to me. "I think the song might've... scared her a bit. She left. I saw Chris outside. I think she got a ride with him."

Chris is our local cabbie. He's dedicated to his job and somehow always seems to appear when you need him. Apparently, that worked for Kennedy tonight. *Fuck.* Scaring her is the last thing I wanted. After that almost-kiss in the kitchen, I didn't think I would.

It doesn't matter. Nothing matters besides getting to Kennedy.

"I've gotta go," I say.

"Yeah, probably a good plan."

"Are you coming?"

"Nah. I'll catch a ride back. Maybe call Chris," he says with a dry laugh. Then he looks at me seriously. "Go get her."

Without another thought, I dash for the door, running down the block and jumping into the driver's seat of my 4Runner. Thankfully, my house is only twelve minutes from the bar. Unfortunately, that feels like an eternity. Especially as I replay every moment with Kennedy from the past few days, leading to this. Over and over I go through it all, each time ending up at the same place. I don't understand why she'd be scared. Unless everything finally caught up to her.

Shit.

When I get to my house, I let out a sigh of relief seeing the lights on inside. Rushing out of my car, I run across the front yard and up the porch steps. My heart thrums as I swing the door open. "Kend? Kennedy? Are you here?"

"Kitchen," she calls, like nothing at all is wrong.

Now I'm just fucking confused.

I slip off my shoes and force myself to slow down. Taking a few deep breaths, I make my way down the hall like everything is normal, and I didn't just drive home like my pants were on fire.

When I get to the kitchen, the fridge is open, obscuring Kennedy from view for a moment. Until she closes the door and spins to face me, smiling brightly.

Oh, and she's naked.

Stark fucking naked in my kitchen.

My brain is working overtime to comprehend everything.

She looked uncertain while I was singing. She's naked. *Then I got off the stage.* She's naked. *She and Justin were arguing.* She's still naked. *He said she ran out.* Holy fuck, she's naked. *I raced home and then saw her* standing here naked. And now she's strolling toward me. Her hand is on my chest and she. Is. Naked.

"Kend, what's going on?" my voice is so high and raspy I barely recognize it. She smiles as she runs her hand down my chest. "I thought you left."

"I did," she says with a laugh.

"No. I thought you left because you were scared or upset."

"Oh," she says dramatically, her smile growing. "No. I just needed a head start. And then for you to hurry back here. Justin was playing along."

"Oh." *Oh.* I slowly run my fingers through the hair at the side of her face. "And that's why you're naked?"

She bites her lip. "It's the fantasy, right? You made your move. This is mine."

I search her eyes. "*You* are the fantasy. *This* isn't all I want. You know that, right?"

"I know," she says quickly. "It's not all I want, either. But it's the fun part." She shivers. "Or it was. I'm getting cold now."

"Well, we can't have that." I quickly pull my shirt off, then put it over her head. She stares at me for a second, so I smile, finally feeling like myself again. "Put your arms in like a good girl."

Her eyes widen slightly, but she does it, then immediately hits me with a pout.

"Why'd you do that?"

Chuckling, I say, "Two reasons. One, you just said you were cold."

"And two?" she asks breathily.

Stepping closer, I trace my finger down her jawline. "Two, I don't want to kiss you for the first time with you standing there naked. If I do that, I'll rush. All I'll be able to think about is doing more, and I want to savor this." Letting my lips follow the path my finger took, I kiss the line of her jaw, to her chin. Then lift my lips and look into her eyes before wrapping my hand around her neck and slowly pressing my lips to hers.

The second our lips meet, everything becomes clear. Everything I want. Everything I need. Everything I've been missing. Fire fills my heart as sparks of electricity crack around us. "Kend," I groan against her lips.

She slides her hand up my chest to the side of my neck, her fingers brushing through the hair at the base as she pulls my lips tighter to hers, deepening our kiss. Wrapping my hands under her ass, I lift her up and set her on the counter, leaning into her. Then her tongue glides over my bottom lip, and without thought, I open my mouth and plunge my tongue into her mouth, swallowing the tiny yelp she lets out at the forcefulness of my movements.

Her fingers curl into my hair as she melts into the kiss, playing along, teasing me like she's done all damn week. Her tongue is like a drug, every stroke, twist, and swirl taking me higher. I'm hooked on her. This endless high. Everything I've ever wanted is right here in this kiss.

But when she reaches for the button of my jeans, I rest my hand over hers, then slowly pull away, chest heaving. She licks her lips as she gazes into my eyes.

"How long?" I ask.

"What?"

"How long have you wanted this?"

She smiles sheepishly. "A long time. What about you?"

I rest my head against hers, letting out a short laugh. "A long time. God, we're idiots."

She shrugs. "Maybe. But it was a lot to risk." Her voice is hushed and vulnerable.

Threading my fingers through her hair, I look deep into her dark whiskey eyes.

"No more risk. This is what I want. You. Us."

"Me too."

"Thank God," I say with a relieved laugh.

We stare at each other for a moment longer, then our lips crash together again in a ferocious, wild kiss. This time, when she reaches for the button of my jeans, I let her undo it. A second later, they're around my ankles and the rock-hard boner I'm sporting is resting between her thighs. Stepping out of my jeans, I rock against her, and she groans.

Smiling against her lips, I slide my hands under the shirt I put on her and slowly lift it up, pulling my lips off hers as I sweep the shirt over her head and toss it on the floor.

"Warmer now?" I ask.

"Definitely."

"Good." I kiss her hard, then work my lips down her neck. Her head drops back as she drags her fingers across my shoulders.

It's good I put my shirt on her earlier. I can barely contain myself now that she's naked again. And damn, I want to take my time. How long have I wanted more with her? To touch her like this? To kiss across her chest and set her skin prickling with goosebumps.

"Devon," she breathes as my mouth moves lower, licking over the curve of her breast then flicking at her nipple with my tongue. Her hands move up to my hair, threading the curls and tugging as I sweep my lips over to her other breast, this time pulling the nipple between my teeth.

She moans again, and my cock strains against the thin fabric of my boxer briefs.

"Devon?"

"Hm?"

"Can you call me a good girl again?"

Jesus fuck.

"You like when I call you a good girl?"

"Mhm," she mumbles as I tweak her nipple between my thumb and forefinger.

Kissing up her neck, I whisper in her ear, "You liked it when I called you that earlier?" Grazing one hand down her thigh, I continue. "Did it make you wet? Were you hoping I'd touch you and find out?"

"Ye-es," she gasps as my fingers dance across her inner thigh. "Please."

"Please what?"

"Touch me."

"I am touching you."

"My pussy. God, Devon. Please."

"Well, since you asked nicely." I stroke my finger up her dripping wet center. She cries out in response to my touch. "Mm. Good girl. So fucking wet for me." I brush my thumb over her clit then dip one finger inside her. "Perfect."

"Yes. Oh." She gasps as her fingers dig into my back, but this isn't nearly enough for me. I've wanted more with her for so damn long, and since she's been here, wrapped in my arms, walking around in tiny towels, sleeping in my T-shirts, moaning in the shower, I've dreamed of tasting her.

She groans in frustration when I pull my finger out, but then she watches as I bring that finger to my mouth and suck, licking off her heady flavor.

"Why is that so hot? Holy shit," she groans, lying back on her elbows.

She's right. It is fucking hot. So hot I can't help myself.

With a growl, I squat down and bury my face between her thighs, lapping at her sweet pussy and enjoying her intoxicating flavor.

She squeaks and her ass lifts off the counter, but I grab her thighs and hold her in place, licking and sucking at her clit as she fists my hair.

Letting go of one thigh, I drag a hand over and slowly circle her pussy, inching my finger in a little more each time until it's swirling and pumping deep inside her. She wraps her legs around my back, her thighs clenching against my head as she moans.

Her hips rock into me as I shamelessly devour and finger fuck her, needing to feel her come. Sliding my finger most of the way out, I curl it up, then move in light, fast strokes. She tugs my hair harder as her abs tighten. I suck her clit between my lips in rhythm with my finger pumping into her.

"Yes, right there. Oh. Yes. I'm going to come. Oh..."

She explodes over my face, her creamy flavor covering my hand and coating my tongue.

Slowly, I pull my finger out, but I keep licking until she pushes my head back.

I stand up, then pull her shaking body upright, kissing her forcefully. She melts into me, resting her weight against me as we kiss. When I pull away, I kiss her forehead, then look into her eyes and whisper the magic words, "Good girl."

CHAPTER TWELVE

Kennedy

HOW FAST CAN you have an orgasm when you've just come down from one? Asking because hearing Devon call me "good girl" is the hottest thing in the entire world. I never knew I needed it until he said it earlier and every nerve ending in my body lit on fire. Now it's all I need to hear and whoops, spontaneous orgasm. Well, almost.

Speaking of orgasms, that may have been my best *ever*. Which is saying something because I know my way around my own body. I mean, maybe after a long session, I've had a harder one, but this was different. Because Devon was the one touching me. Licking me.

The fabric of his boxers rubs against my leg and I can't take it anymore. In an instant, I reach out, grab his boxers, and push them down until they slide off his legs and onto the floor, then I grab that hardened muscle and stroke it.

The groan he lets out sends a chill up my spine.

"Kend… fuck."

"That what you want?" I ask playfully.

His eyes darken and his jaw ticks.

"Protection."

"I'm on birth control. Haven't been with anyone else in nine months and my last test six months ago came back clear. You?"

"I'm good too. Got tested a few months back after my last time."

"So, what are you waiting for?"

That sexy half-smile appears, and he grabs my waist with one hand and wraps the other around the side of my neck. Looking into my eyes, he moves closer. His crown brushes my pussy, and I shudder in anticipation.

Then slowly, driving me to the edge of insanity, he pushes into me.

The moan I let out as he goes deeper is loud and unladylike. Good thing Devon's never cared about me being a lady.

"Fuck," he hisses. "Lie back."

I bristle at the jolt of cold as I lean back. The second my back is flush with the counter, he thrusts deeper. Holding onto my shoulder, he pumps in and out, and *holy fuck.*

I fantasized about being with Devon many times, but while I imagined the physical sensations, I never thought twice about the emotional ones. The safety I feel with him, how intensely wanted I feel, the way this physical connection heightens the emotional bond we've had for so many years. I knew sex with Devon would be amazing, but I didn't know it would be this incredible.

Shifting his weight, he leans forward and kisses me. The weight of his body over mine, the feel of his lips pressing into my lips as he moves inside me only deepens my desire for him, the flames burning brightly inside me.

"Devon," I breathe.

"Fuck yes, baby. Keep saying my name. Say it while I own this pussy, while you come on my cock."

"Devon," I say again and he stands up straight, slowing his movements as he breathes deep.

"You feel so damn good, Kend." After a few breaths, he slides one hand up my ribs, to my shoulder, then my neck, fingers flitting through my hair. "I miss your long hair."

"So do I."

"Good. Because I'm going to need you to grow it out again."

"Why?"

"So I can wrap it around my hand and hold you in place while I fuck you."

Jesus damn.

My back slides across the counter as he thrusts in and out, sweat pooling beneath me.

"Why'd you cut it?"

Trying to find my senses between gasps, I mumble, "Because my boss told me it looked unprofessional."

"Fuck him," he grunts.

My wit returns for long enough for me to smirk and say, "I'd rather fuck you."

His burning eyes lock on me as his hand wraps around my neck. His fingers tease the hair at the back as his thumb presses into my throat. He groans as he thrusts again, going deep to the hilt.

He moves his hand from my hip, down my thigh, until his thumb is swirling against my clit. My walls clench around him and my spine tingles. He's sprinting toward the edge with me, his hand in mine as we barrel toward the cliff, ready to jump.

His eyes have clouded over as he struggles to keep control, but I don't want him in control. I want him here, in this moment, with me.

Gliding my hand up the side of his neck, I look into his eyes. "Devon," I whisper.

His gaze returns to me and the slightest smile plays on his lips. His chest rises and falls faster as his pace quickens. I dig my fingers into his shoulder as we move closer and closer to the edge, eyes locked, emotion thick around us until we go tumbling over the cliff together.

He groans loudly, mumbling my name as I cry out his, until we're a breathless heap against his kitchen counter.

He kisses my neck, then lifts me up, carrying me into the living room. He throws a blanket on the floor and sets me down, turns on the gas fireplace, then grabs another blanket and some pillows from the couch before settling in next to me. Gently lifting my head, he slides a pillow behind me, then lies down next to me and covers us with the other blanket.

"You're beautiful, baby," he says, sweeping a hand over my face.

My heart beats wildly at his words. "I've wanted this for so long."

"So have I."

"Why didn't you ever make a move?"

His eyebrows shoot up. "I did. In the pantry."

"That was four days ago."

"I mean when we were fourteen."

"That was you making a move? Seriously? I thought you just wanted to kiss me."

He shakes his head at me. "I wanted to kiss *you*. I wanted you. The kissing was just how I was going about it."

My cheeks go pink. "Oh."

"Why did you stop me?"

"Because those girls showed up. I knew you could have anyone. I didn't want to risk having my heart crushed if I wasn't the girl you chose."

Brushing his thumb over my cheek, he gazes intensely into my eyes. "I would've chosen you every time, Kennedy. Every. Single. Time."

I roll on top of him and kiss him deeply. "Every time?" I mutter against his lips.

"Always. What about you? Why didn't you ever make a move?" He rolls over so we're lying side by side again.

"Like I said, I didn't want to end up with a crushed heart. If that happened, I wouldn't have been able to be around you. It was easier to put you in the friend zone than risk what could happen otherwise."

"I guess I understand that," he says with a sigh. "I can't imagine my life without you in it."

Biting at my lip, I ask, "What happens now?"

"You're mine. All mine."

I laugh at that, at the sweet yet possessive look in his vibrant green eyes. *Horny eyes.*

"And you're mine."

"Damn right I am. I've waited too long for this. I'm all in, Kend. Whatever life brings, I want us to figure it out together."

"Even if my career takes me somewhere else? I'm planning to stay here for the summer and figure out my options, but what happens after that?"

He takes a deep breath. "Like I said, we'll figure it out together. I want to be with you, Kennedy. Wherever that is." I'm still chewing on my lip, so he tilts his head to the side and stares me down. "What?"

"I just don't want you to sacrifice too much for me."

"Nothing involving you would ever be a sacrifice."

"Devon..."

"I'm serious. There will be compromises, but I'm willing to make them. I've spent too much time without you. Especially these last few years." Burying his face in my neck, he rumbles, "I've missed you."

"I've missed you, too. At night, I used to imagine you were in bed with me—" I stop short. Why am I telling him this?

One eyebrow lifts. "In bed with you, huh? Doing what?"

My cheeks heat, and I dip my head.

"Oh no. No way. The answer is not in my pecs." He bounces his pec muscles, making me laugh. "Tell me," he growls.

"Sometimes, I imagined you were there, snuggling with me, like we used to when we camped in the backyard."

"And other times?"

"Other times... I imagined your hand between my legs, your mouth on my chest, or what it would feel like to have you inside me."

"And were you ever *singing* when you did that?"

I pull the blanket up so it's almost covering my face, but he lifts my chin. "Maybe. A lot," I mutter.

He gives me a blazing smile in response. "And how did it compare to the real thing?"

"It didn't. Not at all. I mean, in my mind it was always incredible, but nothing like what just happened." His cocky smile makes me roll my eyes, and I shove his shoulder. "What about you? Did you think of me?"

"All the damn time. I should've felt guilty about it, but I never did."

Trailing my finger up his stomach, I whisper, "And what did you think about?"

His grin grows, and he rolls on top of me. "Oh, I can't tell you that." He kisses my neck. "But I can show you."

"YES, OH, THAT'S PERFECT. FUCK..." I groan and he slams his mouth over mine as we lose ourselves in each other for the third time tonight. We've been lying by the fireplace talking and then getting hot and heavy for the last hour.

I'm mid moan when the front door swings open. "Hello?" Justin calls.

Shit.

Devon immediately rolls off me, but he's still half inside me. He grabs the blanket, which is around our ankles, and pulls it up. Since neither of us have answered Justin, he wanders down the hall, then stops short when he sees us. A wide smile appears on his face, and he strolls over to us and bends down. He lifts the blanket off me just enough to tell I'm not wearing a shirt, then he chuckles and stands back up.

"Well, it's about damn time."

"Justin, we—"

"Nope," he says, holding up his hand. "I don't need to know. I'm just going to go upstairs, put my headphones on, and not leave my room *all night*."

I sputter for words, but nothing comes out.

With a grin, he walks out of the room and toward the stairs. "Have fun!"

Devon buries his head against my shoulder as he laughs.

"God..." I laugh too, then he kisses me.

Justin's footsteps trail up the stairs, then a door shuts.

"Now, where were we?" Devon asks, rolling on top of me again.

AFTER FINISHING our last round downstairs, Devon turned off the fireplace and we made our way to the master. We finished cleaning ourselves up while intermittently kissing and getting ready for bed. I'm exhausted, fully sated, and so fucking happy.

Flicking his lamp off, he slides under the covers and wraps his arms around me, holding me close. My heart's on fire. I've never felt like this before. Peace and safety combined with exhilaration. Like I know exactly what to expect and don't have a clue at all. The best part is the trust. I don't have to wonder how he feels about me anymore. I don't have to worry if he'll be here in the morning or if he won't like the other sides of me. He already knows it all and wants every part of me. And I feel the same about him. Giving in was the hardest part. Now that I have, I see everything I've been missing and realize how ridiculous my fears were.

My eyes grow heavy as I rest my head on his shoulder.

"Night, baby," he whispers, kissing my forehead.

God, I love hearing him call me that.

"Goodnight, babe," I whisper back. "I love you." Then I drift off to sleep.

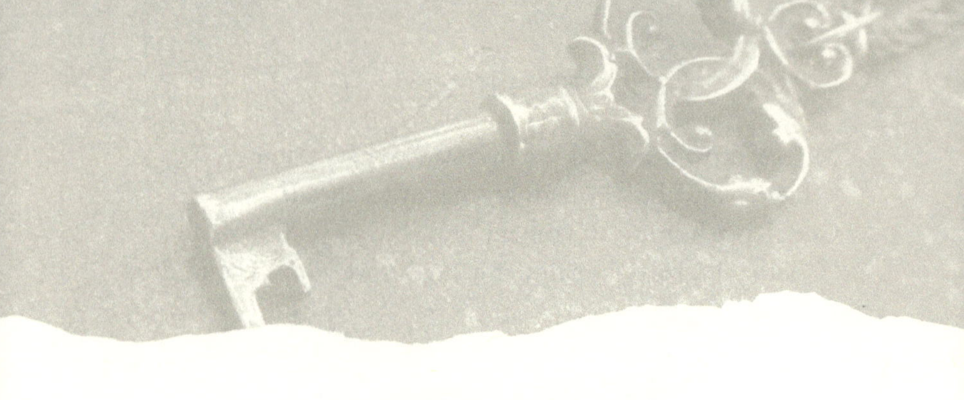

CHAPTER THIRTEEN

SATURDAY

Devon

SUNLIGHT on my face wakes me from a deep sleep. I yawn and reach for Kennedy, finding nothing but an empty bed beside me. Disappointment hits before I smell bacon cooking. Glancing at the clock, I see it's nearly nine-thirty. *Holy shit.* I can't remember the last time I slept this late so easily.

Throwing off the covers, I slip on my sweats and make my way downstairs, all the while thinking about last night. How everything changed. Hoping it wasn't all a dream. Remembering the words she said as she fell asleep.

I love you.

I was afraid to say it to her earlier in the night because I wasn't sure how she felt. I'm still not certain. She said them when she was tired after lots of incredible sex. Should I believe them?

I shake the thought away as I walk down the hall to the kitchen, where Kennedy and Justin are talking and laughing.

"Morning," I say, running a hand through my hair.

Kennedy smiles brightly, then flicks off the burner and walks over to me. "Morning." She presses onto her toes and softly kisses me, and though I want to, I don't set her on the kitchen counter and attack her again. For Justin's sake only.

"You left me alone," I whisper pitifully.

She laughs and shakes her head as she steps back. "I tried to wake you up, but you wouldn't budge." With a twinkle in her eye, she smirks and says, "You were sleeping hard, big boy."

Justin groans over his coffee mug. "Ugh. Can we not do that?"

Kennedy turns to him and shrugs. "Get used to it. We're gonna be gross now."

He shakes his head and walks toward the hallway. "On that note, I'm going to take a nice, long shower. Please, *please* do not let me catch you screwing anywhere. Save it for the bedroom until after I leave, okay?"

"No promises," I call after him, then walk around the kitchen island to where Kennedy is now prepping our sandwiches. Wrapping my arms around her waist, I whisper, "I missed waking up with you in my arms."

"I'm sorry, but you really were out, and I was starving. I've already eaten three slices of bacon. But I promise to stay in bed with you every morning for as long as I'm here."

"All summer long?" I ask, trying not to sound needy, but God, I don't even want to think about her leaving.

She spins to face me, looping her arms around my neck. "All summer... at least."

I lift her onto the counter and lean into her. "And I get to keep you in bed that whole time?"

She swats my shoulder, then groans as I kiss her neck. "How about half the time?"

"I might be agreeable to that."

"Good. Now, I'm still starving. Can we please eat?" My eyes trail down her body and she smacks me again. "I mean food, Devon. You've known me for seventeen years. You know better than to get between me and food."

I chuckle at that and grab the plates sitting next to her. "I suppose so."

Turning around, I walk over to the island and set our plates down. She follows me, sitting down on a stool and looking happily at the breakfast sandwich on her plate before picking it up and taking a massive bite. She groans loudly.

"Good to know where your loyalties lie between sex and food," I say with a laugh.

Mouth still full, she turns to me, chewing several times before swallowing, and daintily wiping her mouth with a napkin like she's not a raging beast when she's hungry. She spins on her stool, one leg crossing over the other. My fingers ache to reach out and touch her velvety skin.

"Sex is fun and beautiful and fucking incredible when it's with the right person." She gives me a little wink. "But food is essential to human life. I don't make the rules, I just follow them." Then she turns back to her sandwich and dives in again.

My head tilts as I watch her chew and swallow another huge bite. Even watching her ravenously eat is sexy.

"Good to know where sex ranks for you," she says between bites.

Leaning over, I test her theory. She may have been ravenously hungry, but she wasn't an equal level of horny. Time to level the playing field. I slowly drag my lips down her neck, occasionally kissing, then sucking the skin into my mouth.

She makes a little mumbly noise, so I keep going, continuing to kiss and suck on her neck while running my other hand up her silky thigh, underneath my T-shirt, until my fingers are brushing the edge of her underwear. She gasps as I graze them over the crotch. Smiling to myself, I pull my hand away, lift my lips from her neck, and turn on my stool, grabbing my sandwich and taking a bite.

She makes a discontented noise and crosses her arms over her chest, glaring at me.

I shrug. "Sorry. I'm hungry."

"No, you're not."

"I am. Starved."

She cocks an eyebrow. "Oh, really?"

Sliding off her stool, she stands next to me, running one hand through my hair and the other over my stomach. She traces my abs, then moves up to my pecs, slowly circling each nipple before rolling them between her thumb and pointer. I didn't realize having my nipples teased would turn me on, but fuck, it does. So much so that I let out a gasp. My sandwich is in my hands in mid-air because I stopped thinking when her skin touched mine.

She leans in and kisses my neck, and I know I've lost this round.

Quickly spinning on my stool, I stand up and pull her to me, giving her a hard kiss.

She's smiling when I pull away.

"So," I rumble, "sex or food?"

With one hand, she grazes my crotch, and with the other, she grabs her breakfast sandwich and takes a bite. "Both."

"You're ridiculous."

"Maybe." She sets her breakfast sandwich back down and wraps her arms around my neck. "But so are you. I love you." My eyes flare at her words and she laughs. "Don't look so surprised. I said it last night, too."

"I know. I just wasn't sure if it was—"

"That post-orgasm glow?" she asks cheekily.

"Something like that."

She squeezes my hand. "I don't expect you to say it back, but it's how I feel, so I wanted to say it."

I laugh lightly, then take her face in my hands, looking into her eyes. "I love you, Kend. I have for a long time. I was just too much of a chicken to say it first."

"Well, I guess I can forgive that, since you did make the first move."

I capture her mouth in a deep kiss, my tongue swirling in her mouth, claiming her.

"Bedroom?" I mumble against her lips.

"Bring the food."

"As you wish, baby."

I grab both of our sandwiches and we dash up the stairs and into the bedroom, where we fully satiate both kinds of hunger.

Kennedy

"THAT WAS SO GOOD," I moan.

Devon rolls his eyes. "Again, you're wounding my ego."

I set the plate to the side and slide back under the covers. "The fact that we had sex *before* we ate should be a big ego boost."

He pulls me into his arms and I rest my head on his chest.

"I guess I'll have to take what I can get."

"Give me a few minutes to digest and I'll give you some more."

"Mm. I love you. And this."

"Just think, if we weren't such chicken shits, we could've been doing this for years."

"Ugh, don't remind me. My dick is so mad at me about that."

I smack his chest. "Good to know sex is all you care about."

He kisses my neck. "You know that's not true. I wish we would've admitted it sooner. Yes, we could have been having years worth of amazing sex, but there have been so many times in the last few years where I wished I had someone by my side. A partner."

"You know," I say softly, "I would've come if you'd called. If you had told me you needed me, I would've been here. I can't read your mind, Dev, but I'm always here for you. That's the one thing that shouldn't be changing from friendship to relationship."

"You were working so hard. I didn't want to ask you to take time away from that."

My brows pinch together. "Well, that's dumb. And whatever happens from here, you better promise me you won't do anything like that again. No more struggling alone. I'm here."

"I love that you're here," he whispers, tugging on my heart-strings and making me want to stay forever. Right now, that's still in the maybe category. I mean, I know no matter what, I want to be with him—physically and in a relationship—but where and what happens next is what I don't know. Frankly, I have no desire to think about it. I want to enjoy this. We waited long enough to get here. I want to live in this stupidly happy, can't-stop-touching-each-other, never-want-to-leave-the-bedroom phase for as long as possible.

"Devon?"

"Hm?"

"The other night, when you were talking about your future—love, marriage, kids—were you talking about me? Us?"

His lips are pressed against the side of my head, and I can feel him smiling.

"Always. You're the one I dreamed of having it all with. I tried for so long to deny it, but I finally gave in after..."

"What?" I ask.

He sighs, then laughs and looks up at the ceiling. "After I called another girl your name in bed."

My eyes widen. "Oh my god. Seriously?"

He nods. "Yep. Not one of my proudest moments, but that's when I knew for sure. Maybe it's what gave me the strength to finally cross the line."

"I'm glad you started... having some fun."

"I'm glad you played along."

"It was fun. Hot. Terrifying," I laugh. "And so hard to resist."

"Funny, that's how I felt when I heard you *singing* in the shower."

I run my hand over my face. "Oh god. I was so freaking embarrassed. But then it turned into another way to tease each other." Tickling my fingers down his stomach, I whisper, "Maybe we should sing together in the shower."

He groans. "That sounds so good."

Pulling me closer, he kisses me deeply. We're a mess of lips and tongues and tangled body parts until my phone begins loudly playing *Stacy's Mom*.

Devon pulls away suddenly and raises his eyebrows. *"Stacy's Mom?* Really?"

"It's Frannie and Hallie. It's an inside joke. We were obsessed with that song in elementary school. We thought it was so funny." I sit up and pull the sheet up so I'm covered, then grab my phone and answer the video call.

"Hello," I say cheerily.

"Is that all you have to say?" Frannie demands.

"Well, I just answered, so... yes?"

"You can't just send a text that says, 'Hey, Devon and I are together,' and then tell us *nothing* else. What is wrong with you?" Hallie yells.

"Sorry." *I'm not.* "I was busy." *Having sex with Devon.*

"I'm sure you were," Hallie says knowingly.

We all giggle. "By the way, Frannie, you have no room to talk. You barely told us anything about Mark until you were home. We didn't even know it was Mark Abbott until it hit the tabloids."

"To be fair, I didn't know that either," Frannie says pointedly, looking off camera.

"Who cares? You love me regardless," Mark yells.

We all laugh at that.

"Well, come on! We need details," Frannie says.

"Right. Uh. Maybe not right now."

Hallie leans in toward the screen. "Hold up. Are you in bed?"

"Perhaps."

"Oh my god, are you like *in bed?*" Hallie asks.

"Mhm. He's going down on me right now."

At this point, Devon, who had been silently listening, leans in and grabs the phone, tilting it toward him. "She's lying. If I was going down on her, she wouldn't be able to talk."

Hallie and Frannie shriek with laughter.

"He's right," I whisper. "Anyway... there's not much to tell that you don't know."

"Bullshit!" Hallie says. "What the hell happened between our last video call and this one?"

"Uh... tell you what, I'll give you the Cliff Notes. We almost kissed. He sang me Lee Brice. I got naked in the kitchen. Lots of sex. Oh, and I think there was some food in there somewhere. Anyway," I say as Devon kisses my neck, "I should go. Love you guys. Talk soon!"

"Have fun being gross," Hallie calls as Frannie laughs.

Devon grabs the phone from my hand and hangs up, then drops it onto the bedside table before climbing out of bed.

"Where are you going?" I pout.

He holds out his hand. "To shower. I thought we were going to do a duet."

My eyes light and I jump out of bed, running ahead of him into the bathroom.

DEVON and I are whispering and being handsy as we walk into the kitchen.

Again, Justin groans.

"Should I just leave early? Let you two have the house?"

"Don't you dare!" I protest. Dropping Devon's hand, I walk over to Justin. "I'm sorry we're being gross. We're just happy, but I don't want you to leave. I've missed you too. Just not like I missed him." He gives me a massive pout. "Aw, are you jealous?"

Grabbing a glass from the cabinet, I fill it with water from the dispenser on the fridge.

"Well, that is why he became your friend in the first place. He wanted to..." Devon trails off, wiggling his eyebrows.

I spin back to face Justin and smack his chest. "Shut up. No. You became friends with me so you could screw me?"

"Believe me, I got over that urge *very* quickly."

"Rude," I say, taking a drink of my water.

"Hey, I stuck around for a lot longer than I would've if I'd hooked up with you. And now here we are. Ten years later. You two are finally together, and I have to hear you fucking in the shower."

"Nah. We were just singing," Devon deadpans.

I choke on my water, spitting half of it all over the floor.

Justin's eyebrows go up, then he shakes his head. "Wow. What a tough code to crack."

Devon is laughing as I wipe the spit water off my chin.

"This is going to be a thing forever now, isn't it?" I ask.

"Probably." Devon grins at me.

Whatever, let it haunt me till the day I die, because I'm too utterly happy to give a shit about anything else right now.

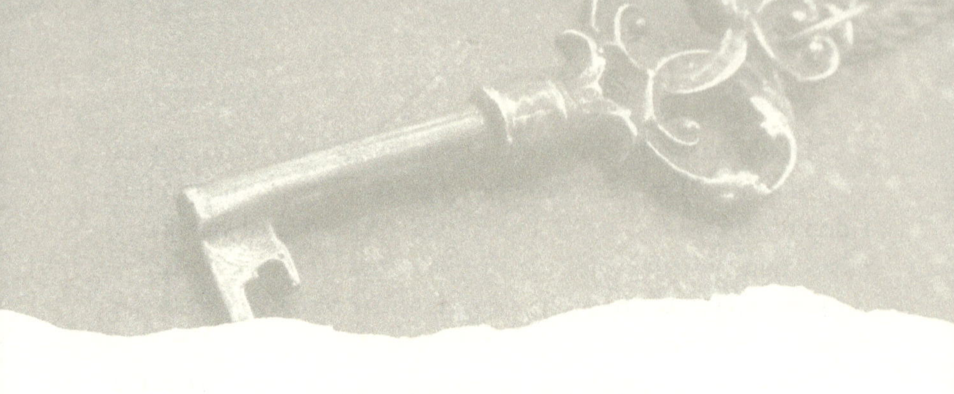

CHAPTER FIFTEEN

MONDAY

Kennedy

AFTER A WEEKEND SPENT IN BED, enjoying good food, annoying Justin, and being fawned over by Devon's mom, we're on our way to the inn to start the week, and sipping on lattes Devon made before we left the house.

This whole me making breakfast, him making coffee thing is the perfect balance. Adding sex makes things even better. It has me thinking about what he said on Friday. I can't believe it's only been a few days. It feels like forever. Maybe because so much of our relationship is rooted in a beautiful friendship. Which is the reason I'm thinking about what he said about wanting me to stay.

My plan was to go back to New York and look for a job, but even before Devon and I finally crossed the line, I had decided to stay here longer. There's something about Brighton that's pulling me in, but I'm not sure if it's just the break from my usual reality. Devon being here, of course, also plays into what I do from now on, and I'm starting to wonder if I want to go back to New York or look for a job in San Francisco, instead. Claire might have some connections. Or maybe I should consider somewhere else entirely. Somewhere Devon and I could go together. If he'd be open to that. Maybe it's too soon to think about it, but it's on my mind, regardless.

"Ready for the day?" Devon asks, pulling me out of my thoughts.

I chuckle at that. "Yeah. I'm ready for Gladys to give us her most knowing smile."

"Yeah, she's been hoping for this for a while."

"I think everyone has."

My phone rings, startling me, and I look down at it. Seeing a New York number I don't recognize, my brow furrows. It could be spam, but since it's my area code, I answer.

"Hello, this is Kennedy Baker."

Devon laughs at my formality, so I smack his stomach.

He turns up the drive to the inn as a familiar voice says, "Hi, Kennedy. This is Eric Williams." My former editor at the job I was laid off from last week.

"Uh, hi, Eric. How are you?"

"I'm good. And you?"

"Good, thanks."

"I'm sure you're wondering why I'm calling. I'd hoped HR would've reached out to you, but apparently, they didn't."

"Uh, no."

"It turns out you weren't the first to file a report against Mike Hunt. They investigated and quickly found several other situations in which he'd been inappropriate with staff. He's been let go, along with a few of his protégés, who were found assisting him and engaging in similar behavior. There's a huge restructuring happening in the company now, and I'll be taking over his position. I'm setting up my senior editors, and I'd really like one of them to be you. Of course, I can't just give you the job, but if you're interested, I'd love for you to come in and meet with the managing department heads and our editor-in-chief."

What the freaking hell?

"I..."

"Listen, Kennedy, I know it was awful how you were treated, but the other department heads and I, along with HR, are working hard to make sure that doesn't happen again."

"I appreciate that," I say, finding my voice. "What would the job entail?" I know generally what senior editors do, but I want to hear some specifics before I get excited. Even though my stomach is in my throat in a mix of excitement and nerves. Not sure why I'm nervous, though.

"My intention would be to have you as senior editor over-seeing book reviews primarily, along with some television and movies. You'd get to interview authors. I know you want some meatier stories, so I'll do my best to get you more of that too, and it's possible that moving into another department would be an option, eventually."

Devon looks at me curiously as he parks the car.

"When would you need me to come in?" I ask hesitantly. Generally speaking, this is where I want to go in my career, but something in my gut feels off.

"We'd need you to come in this week."

"Is there any way I could do a video meeting? I'm in California currently."

"I'm sorry, but they want to meet with everyone in person before final decisions are made. If you're interested, it would have to be this week. This would be a big step for you, Kennedy."

The dream job.

So, why do I feel hesitant?

"We're scheduling people on Wednesday and Thursday. Could you do either of those days?"

I bite my lip. That would be before the reunion. I'd have to fly out and fly back. And I have the book club on Tuesday night.

"Can you hold on a moment?"

"Sure."

I mute my phone and look at Devon.

"What is it?"

"My old job wants me back. They fired the guy who let me go and they want to make me a senior editor—but only if I can interview in person on Wednesday or Thursday."

"This week?"

"Uh huh."

"Do you want to do it?"

"I don't know. I would need to fly out and back before the reunion."

"That's not what I asked you." He sweeps some hair off my cheek and looks into my eyes. "I asked if you want to."

I bite at my bottom lip. "I feel like I should. It's a really good opportunity. What I've been working toward."

"Then you have to do it."

"But Devon, what about..." I look around the parking lot and up at the inn. "All of this? Me staying the summer? Us?"

He leans in and softly kisses my lips. "The inn will always be here, and as fun as a summer here together sounds, you can't pass up a good career move."

"And us?"

"Babe, you have nothing to worry about with us. We'll figure it out. I'm never letting you go."

I nod slowly. "Okay. I'll go. But I'm not sure if it's... the right move."

"We can figure that out after, but it won't even be an option if you don't go."

"Yeah."

I unmute my phone and put it back against my ear.

"What's the latest you have on Wednesday?"

"I can do as late as 4:45. Does that work?"

"Put me down. I'll be there."

"Sure thing. I hope you'll consider this. It'll be a big step for you on your career path. You deserve this."

"Thanks," I say, stomach twisting.

"Of course. Take care, Kennedy. See you soon."

"Yes. Thanks. Take care. Bye."

The line disconnects, and I slowly lower my phone from my ear and turn to look at Devon.

"Hey, you okay? Because you don't look it. You just got an incredible job opportunity."

"I know, but..." *I'm enjoying my time here.* "It happened sooner than I was expecting. Hell, I wasn't expecting it at all."

I should be excited. This is my dream job. He's supporting me. But there's this nagging in my stomach, and I kind of want to cry.

He leans in and kisses me, and I finally relax. "I'm proud of you. You should be proud, too. You've worked hard for this."

"I have. And I am. It's just... after being fired or laid off, whatever, all those hours I put in, all the effort, it started to feel like a waste. In some ways, it still does. This used to be exactly what I wanted. And it is... tantalizing, but I don't feel excited about it like I thought I would."

"Let it sink in. It's okay if you're not sure yet, but don't let a great option pass you by, either."

"Are you sure you're okay with it?"

"I never want to hold you back from following your dreams."

That wasn't what I asked. And I'm not sure this is my dream anymore.

"Okay."

He scrunches his nose. "Hey, I told you we'd figure this all out together, and I mean it. Now, you are way too grumpy and sad. You just got an awesome job opportunity. And we are finally a couple." He kisses my cheek, then my lips. "Or did I not prove that enough this weekend?"

"You did some good proving," I chuckle.

"Then show me your excited face."

I flash a smile. And I do feel a little better. A little more excited. Dream opportunity. Now I've got the dream guy. Could I really have everything I wanted?

"Come on," he says, opening his car door. "Let's go tell Gladys."

I smile as he climbs out of the car. Not everyone who falls for their best friend gets so lucky. Hell, I'm lucky to have him in the first place. To have his love, too? That's the best thing ever.

GLADYS WAS both unsurprised and thoroughly excited to hear we were together. Shockingly, Devon's mom had not already told her. She did, however, text my mom, but thankfully, I'd already texted her, Frannie, and Hallie over the weekend to fill them in.

Now I'm sitting at the desk with Gladys, half looking at reunion stuff and half overthinking everything.

"Who are they now?" I ask, looking through a pile of papers about the reunion.

"Yes, that's the theme. Didn't you read your invitation?"

I laugh. "No. I think it showed up in my email, but Devon had already told me about it and I'd taken the time off, so I just ignored it and moved on."

Gladys shakes her head. "Well, that is the theme. There's going to be a slideshow with pictures of you back in high school and again now. I'm sure you would've been asked to provide some had you looked at the email. Devon handled that for you, though."

"Hopefully he chose some good ones," I say, blowing my hair off my face as I look back at the pile of reunion stuff—mostly notes from Gladys and Devon about the decorations, food, and layout.

I read the words again. *Who are they now?*
Great question.
My mind drifts back. Who did I think I was going to be?

I sneak out the side door of the school, doing my best to be inconspic-uous. I don't know why. It's not like I've never skipped class before. And it's the back half of senior year. Nothing important is happening, anyway.

I head for the nearby tree line and find Devon leaning against a tree.

"Hey," he says, his green eyes vibrant as usual.

"Hey."

He wraps his arm around me in a half hug like he hasn't seen me five times today.

"Claire coming?"

"Right here," she says from behind me.

"Anyone see you?" I ask.

She snorts. "No. And trust me, we're the least of everyone's problems. The assistant principal just caught two people fucking in a car in the parking lot. There's a whole crowd out front which made it easy to sneak away."

"I don't understand the appeal of fucking in the school parking lot, but whatever," I say.

Claire shakes her head. "Dumbasses are probably going to be expelled four months before we graduate."

"Nah. It's too much paperwork to expel anyone," Devon says as we walk down a worn trail between the trees that leads to a small parking lot where Devon's old minivan is parked. We all climb into the back.

"Four more months," I say. "Can you believe we're almost done with high school?"

"Thank fucking God. I'll be out of here the second that diploma is in my hand," Claire says.

"I think we're going back to New York," I admit for the first time.

Devon stares at me. "Why didn't you tell me?"

I shrug. "We're still going to college together. I know my parents are going back. I'm just not sure when."

"They're selling the house?" Devon asks.

"Yep. I overheard them talking about it last night. They haven't officially told me yet, but they're going to. It doesn't surprise me. My dad has been working long distance for a New York company for years. They were just being nice enough not to move me again."

"Like they did for a job your dad ended up hating?" Claire rolls her eyes.

I bump my leg against hers. "Hey, it worked out okay." My eyes go to Devon. "My life wouldn't be the same without you two."

"Oh, god. Please do not get sentimental on me. You two can hold each other and cry when I'm not around. I'd rather scrape my ear canal with something sharp."

Devon chuckles as I shake my head. "Fine then. Where do you think we'll be in ten years?" I ask.

"Not living here if there's a god above," Claire says.

"No, you'll be too busy being a boss bitch CEO of some massive company," Devon says.

"I don't know about massive, but I want to run my own company," Claire says. Then she points at me. "And you'll be the bigshot journalist writing about it. And all your TV and book reviews, like you do for the school paper."

I smile at that. "That's the dream. Who knows what journalism will be like at that point, but hopefully, I'll get into one of the big online news sites. Writing, editing, bringing people together and starting conversation." I'm nearly giddy as I say the words. "Assuming I get there."

"You will," Devon says. "You're too good at it not to succeed." I scoff, but he doubles down. "I'm serious, Kend. You will."

"And what about you, model boy?" Claire teases. "You going to take the underwear world by storm?"

Devon smiles coyly. "Maybe. Don't worry, I'll send you some signed photos to hang in your office."

"Good. Cause we better still be friends."

"Ooh, now who's getting sentimental?" I tease.

"Yeah, yeah. I will miss you, assholes, but we'll keep in touch regularly while we take the world by storm."

"Here's to that," I agree.

Writer and editor. Rising through the ranks. That was the dream. It all seemed so simple at the time. Go for what you want and get it. Of course, I also thought I'd understand everything and have my life perfectly together at twenty-eight. Cue the laugh track. Life slams a few doors in your face, tosses you around, and you have to figure out the new path all while still not knowing a goddamn thing.

"Is it okay if I don't know what I want to be when I grow up?" I ask Gladys.

She turns from the computer, dropping her glasses off her nose and letting them hang from the chain around her neck as she smiles at me.

"I didn't know, either. I grew into it. You don't have to know right now. Or ever. You can do whatever feels right. It's not about what you do, it's about who you are. Figure that out and let it guide you. Who are you, Kennedy Baker? Who do you want to be? And will taking that job in New York help you be that person?"

Good question.

"No one else can choose your life for you. Take your time, look inside yourself, and you'll find your way. You have too beautiful of a heart not to."

With a wink, she pops her glasses back on and turns to the computer again.

Who am I? Who do I want to be?

I'm still not sure I know the answers to either of those questions.

Devon walks toward the desk, smiling brightly.

Right now, all I know is I'm happy.

That's half the battle, right?

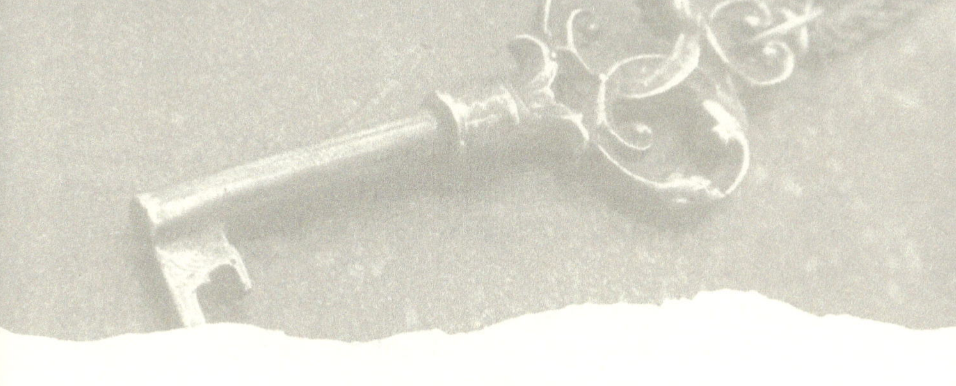

CHAPTER SIXTEEN

Devon

"HERE, LET ME HAVE THE CRUTCHES," I say to my dad as he settles into the passenger seat of my 4Runner.

He hands them to me, and I shut the door behind him, then put the crutches in the back seat before making my way around to the driver's side and climbing in.

"So, where are we going for lunch?" Dad asks.

The man has always been a foodie, and since we're in San Francisco for his specialist appointment, lunch at a new restaurant or some place he's never been to is next on the agenda.

After I dropped Kennedy off at the inn—and made sure she was okay since that phone call surprised her—I left to pick up my dad for his appointment. Anything more than a short car ride is rough on my mom's hips and low back, so she avoids them when she can.

"You tell me. I found a good sandwich shop, a hot dog and ice cream place, and a hole-in-the-wall Korean restaurant."

"Korean sounds wonderful," Dad says. Which I was expecting, but I wanted him to have options. He loves Asian food. He and my mother spent six months traveling through Asia after college.

"Had a feeling you'd say that."

"Let's be sure to get some takeout for your mother. And Kennedy, too. How's she doing?"

"Okay. She actually got a call this morning about a job at the company she was working for in New York."

"The one that laid her off?"

"Yep. Turns out they fired the guy who did that. She made an impression on one of her editors who wants to hire her back and promote her."

"That's wonderful. I'm sure she's thrilled."

"Not really, actually. She seemed like she was about to have a panic attack when she was talking to him. I think being laid off this last time left her wondering if this is still the career path she wants. She also has to fly back to New York to interview, which she's not excited about. She's going back on Wednesday morning, doing her interview that afternoon, then flying back here Thursday."

"That does make it more stressful."

I navigate us out of the parking lot and onto the busy San Francisco streets.

"Definitely. I think she's worried about how it'll affect us, too."

"Ah. And if she got the job and wanted it, would you go to New York with her?"

I swallow hard, guilt coursing through me. I want to be with Kennedy wherever she is, and I want her to have the world, but leaving my parents—who I moved back here to care for—doesn't feel great.

"Most likely. But I'd take some time and make sure the inn was in good hands. I'd still oversee everything, though. And I'd make sure you and Mom had someone to rely on full time, and I'd come back frequently—"

"Devon," Dad says sternly. "Do not use my condition or your mother's as a reason not to leave here. You have to live your life."

"But—"

"No," he says sharply. "No buts. Life is too short and too precious to be wasted or put on hold. I know it all too well. Your mother and I have had to face that reality much sooner than we would've liked. I don't want that for you. Take chances, live your life. If you love her, go to New York with her. Or Chicago. London. Paris. Shang-Hai. I don't care. Live. The inn will be fine, and so will we. Promise me."

I stare at him for a moment, then nod. "I promise."

"Good. Now, how long does it take to get to this restaurant? I'm starving."

"TODAY HAS BEEN CRAZY," Kennedy says, walking out of the bathroom in my T-shirt.

"How are you feeling about the interview now?"

She shrugs as she walks over to the bed and climbs in. "I don't know. I'm excited, but I'm still not sure about it, either. Regardless, it means a lot that they're even considering me, but I'm a little bummed the real world came for us so soon. I like the honeymoon period."

"So do I," I rumble, kissing her neck. "In a perfect world, I'd have you all to myself all the time."

She drags her hand up my bare stomach. "Well, I guess we'll have to make the most of the time we have right now." She leans over and kisses my neck as her hand moves lower. "And right now, I'm yours. All yours." She dips her hand inside my boxers and strokes my cock, bringing it to life in an instant.

"I love you," I mutter against her lips, then graze my hand up her thigh.

"I love you too," she breathes as she shimmies out of her underwear.

A moment later, I'm buried deep inside her and everything else washes away.

CHAPTER SEVENTEEN

TUESDAY

Kennedy

"OH MY GOD!" Lily squeals, as she walks over to where Claire and I are standing, a signed book and a photo with Justin in her hands. "You are incredible! I can't believe I got to meet him."

Claire snickers.

"What? You don't think he's hot?" Lily demands.

Claire shrugs. "I've had hotter."

"Why did you even come?" I ask with a laugh.

"To heckle, obviously. And I wanted to see what my potential clientele is."

"What do you do?" Lily asks.

Claire stares at her for a second, but I elbow her before she can say something snarky.

"I'm the CEO of Bloom Beauty. We have a store here in Brighton, and I want to reach the local market more." She gestures around at all the women fawning over Justin. "And this is my market."

Lily's eyes are wide. "Oh my god! I love that store. I didn't even know there was one in Brighton! I always order online. God, I've been paying shipping this whole time."

Claire's look is somewhere between amused and annoyed. "Yep. We have one here. Frankly, I need to get more people in the door. Kennedy suggested doing an event there. Maybe a girls' night in, wine and facials kind of thing? Possibly with makeup tutorials—"

Lily grabs Claire's arm, and I bristle. Claire isn't exactly the touchy-feely type. And Lily is the type who doesn't care what type you are.

"That sounds like so much fun! I know a lot of the women in this group would love it. Probably some of the moms at school, too. But they kind of scare me."

"I'm surprised anything scares you," Claire says dryly.

"Anyway," Lily continues as if Claire hadn't spoken, "you totally have a market here. You just need to utilize it. I think Kennedy's right. Events are a great way to do that. Plus advertising at local businesses. Everyone finds out everything here through word of mouth." She snaps her fingers. "I could put together a little marketing plan for you."

Claire is about to snort and roll her eyes when I flare mine, reminding her this is a potential customer. Clearing her throat, she simply says, "I have a marketing team."

"Well, duh," Lily says. "But they're looking at the broad markets, not the individual ones. I know this area, and I know marketing. I have a bachelor's degree in it. Right now, all I use it for is helping get people in the door at the library, but that's not too hard. I'd love to do more. Help you out."

I look between the two, thoroughly amused at this unlikely turn of events.

"Okay," Claire says warily. "Sure, let's talk." She pulls out a card and hands it to her. "Call me tomorrow. The first thing you can do is help Kennedy plan an event at the store for some time next month." Claire turns to me. "Assuming, of course, that you'll still be here then."

I wince when she says it. Lily's eyes go wide again.

"Why wouldn't you be here?"

"I have an interview in New York tomorrow, but I'll be back on Thursday. I'm not sure yet if I want the job or not."

"Oh," Lily says. Just when I think she'll be disappointed, she smiles. "Well, if it's what you want, I hope you get it. I'll just have to become your number one social media stalker if you leave."

I'd laugh at that, but I know she's one hundred percent serious.

"Hey, babe," Devon croons, strolling over to me and wrapping an arm around my waist. I swear, the longer he's around Justin, he starts to pick up some of his southern accent.

Lily goes rigid, eyes massive, and cheeks pink.

"What's happening right now?" Claire asks.

"Nothing. Don't worry about it. Lily, why don't you go see if Cindy needs any help."

Lily stares for a moment longer, then coughs. "Right. Yeah. I'll see you later." She scurries away.

Devon watches in confusion. "Uh, what was that?"

I lower my voice and lean in toward him. "No telling, but she saw the underwear ad you did with Justin back in the day. You had quite the effect on her."

Claire lets out a loud laugh. "Fucking priceless. At least we know how to shut her up now."

"Hey, be nice," I say.

Her brow furrows. "I'm not sure I know what that word means."

I roll my eyes at her, then look over at Devon. "Did you need something?"

"A kiss," he says, pressing his lips to mine as Claire makes a gagging noise in the background. "And Justin was hoping you'd help with the reading. He says it's more entertaining when he has someone to read the female parts, and he rejected the idea of me using a high-pitched voice."

"Tell him I'm in as long as he doesn't choose a sex scene."

"I'd kick his ass if he did. I'll let him know. Love you," he rumbles, kissing my cheek as he walks away.

I look over my shoulder at him, lost in the gooey feelings I have for him and how perfect his ass looks in the jeans he's wearing, until Claire pinches my arm.

"Ow. What was that for?"

"You're obsessed." My smile does nothing to discourage that thought. "I'm surprised you're going back to New York."

"Just for the interview. Do you think I shouldn't since I'm with Devon?"

"No. You know I'd never tell you that. I want you to pursue whatever future you want. I'm just surprised you still want that, I guess. Ever since you've been here, you've been stupidly happy. Every time I saw you in New York, you weren't like this. You're..." she makes a face, "glowing."

"Oh. I don't know about glowing, but I'm having a good time here. It's a complete change from the rest of my life. That's part of why I'm going back. I need to see how I feel in the real world, not the Brighton bubble."

Her brow furrows. "So, you're going back to see if you can be less happy in New York for a job you *might* want?"

"Jeez. When you say it like that..."

"Look, I'm not trying to discourage you. If you want it, grab it by the balls and go get it. Don't give up. I guess I was just surprised when you told me because you and Devon are happy as fuck, and while I'm not dying for an epic love story, you two are perfect." She clears her throat. "I just want you to be happy, wherever that might be."

"Aw, look at you being sentimental."

"I hate it. Stop making me do it."

"I don't know what New York will bring, but it shouldn't change things between Devon and me," I say, though in the pit of my stomach, I know it will. If I get that job, I'm not sure what'll happen. If he'll move to New York or if we'd have to do long distance for a while. Frankly, I've been trying not to think about it since he's being really supportive and said we'll figure it out together.

"So he's willing to move out there?"

I look over my shoulder at where Devon is laughing with Justin, Gladys—who we convinced to come tonight—and his mom.

"Yeah," I say, turning back to Claire and trying to exude confidence. "I think so."

Claire gives a slow nod, which I know means she's not confident in my answer.

Fair, because neither am I. But before I can think about it anymore, Justin calls me over to read with him. As I walk past Devon, he gives me a little swat on the butt and a wink, making me temporarily forget all my concerns.

Devon

"GOD, YOU WERE SEXY TONIGHT," I mutter, kissing Kennedy's neck the second she joins me in bed.

"Was I?"

I lift my lips off her neck and look at her.

"Hell yes. You were happy, full of life, and charming everyone. You're a natural people person, and there's nothing sexier than seeing you in your element. Not to mention you getting up and reading that chapter with Justin. Wasn't even a sex scene, but hell, it turned me on."

"Me flirting with Justin gets you off? Maybe we should have him join us tonight," she teases.

Shaking my head, I pin her to the bed and crawl on top of her.

"Mm. I don't think so." Dipping my head down, I run my lips up her neck. "You're mine, remember? All mine. Or do I need to remind you?"

"All yours? Hm. I'm not sure I recall signing up for that."

Heat floods my body and my dick springs to life. The challenge in her voice sets me off, and I'm ready to play.

In a quick motion, I climb off her, then flip her over, pinning her to the bed again. Before I get started, I lean down and whisper in her ear. "You okay?"

She nods. "I'll tell you if I don't like something."

"Good," I breathe, then I sit back on my heels and rub my hand over her ass, feeling the warmth of her skin before lifting my hand and spanking her.

A soft cry of pain mixed with pleasure spills out of her mouth.

Grabbing a wrist in each hand, I pin her arms behind her back, holding both wrists with one hand as I slap her ass again, a little harder this time.

"You don't remember who you belong to? Good girls remember."

"Maybe I don't want to be good."

Taking a fist full of her hair, I turn her head to the side. "So you want to be fucked like a bad girl?"

"Yes," she hisses, wiggling her ass toward me.

My girl likes a little roleplaying. I could get used to this. I've had fantasies, but never been with anyone long enough to want to explore them. With Kennedy, I want to try it all.

Backing up, I grab her thighs and push them forward so her ass lifts into the air, then lie flat on my back and slide my head between her legs, lifting them so she's sitting on my face.

"Oh my god," she gasps as I lick up her center.

Holding her thighs, I eat her sweet pussy like it's my last meal. Every moan is an ego boost. Every gasp of pleasure and trembling muscle urges me on. She moves with my tongue, riding my face until she's so close every muscle in her body has tightened up.

That's when I stop licking, softly kiss her clit, and slide out from under her.

"Wha—what are you doing?" she whines.

"You think you get to come? Bad girls don't get to come until I say."

She lets out an exasperated groan.

I smack her ass again. "That's your incentive to be a good girl," I whisper.

Pushing onto my knees, I kneel behind her and grab her hips. Lining up at her center, I thrust into her, going as deep as I can.

"Ah!"

"Still good?" I whisper.

"Mhm," she whimpers.

Smiling to myself, I say, "Good. Grab that headboard so I can fuck you properly."

With deep breaths, she pushes up on trembling arms, then grabs the headboard.

I go deep again, then hold her in place as I fuck her with hard, punishing strokes. Her cries of pleasure and pain urge me on, and I go faster, harder until her walls tighten around me. Using all the self-control in my body, I pull out and sit back.

She groans in frustration.

"Not yet."

Leaning forward again, I run my hands up her arms, kissing her neck as I lift her hands off the headboard.

I rub my palms across her stomach, then up to her breasts, squeezing them firmly as her head drops back against my shoulder. I rock my cock against her ass, giving me some minor relief.

She moans again, and I sink my teeth into her neck. I pull away slowly, tugging on her skin. Then I spin her around and toss her on her back so she's lying beneath me. Her dripping pussy makes my cock ache.

Slowly, I drag my hand up her stomach and chest until I'm at her neck. I raise an eyebrow and she gives a slight nod, so I wrap my hand around her neck at the same time I thrust my cock into her as hard as I can.

She whimpers and digs her fingernails into my back while pressing her heels into my ass, begging for more.

Pressing my hand against her throat, I pump in and out fast

and hard. With my other hand, I tease her clit, getting as close to it as I can without touching it.

"Please…"

"Are you ready to behave?"

"Yes. Yes. Just please… let me come."

"Who do you belong to?"

"You," she cries.

"Say my fucking name, Kennedy."

"Devon! Oh…" I slide my thumb over her clit and rub a circle around it. "Yes," she cries out. "Yes, yes. Devon…" she whimpers, fisting the sheets as I drive into her and rub her clit until she erupts, her gorgeous body shaking beneath mine. Her eyes roll back as she lets out a choked breath, and I can't hold back anymore.

"Kend… oh, fuck, baby. You feel so good. Your pussy is so tight. Perfect." I kiss her neck as I fill her up.

"Does that mean I'm a good girl again?" she purrs.

"You're perfect," I say breathlessly, collapsing next to her and wrapping her in my arms. "I love you."

"I love you too. I don't want to leave tomorrow."

"I know. But you've got to shoot your shot, babe."

"You just shot yours," she teases.

I shut her up with a kiss. "Didn't hear any complaining."

"Only bad girls would do something like that." She kisses my nose, then winks at me and climbs out of the bed, swaying her hips as she walks to the bathroom.

I don't want her to leave tomorrow, either. Even a night without her feels like too long, but I push the thought away, refusing to let anything ruin how incredible tonight has been.

A few minutes later, she's nestled in my arms as we both drift off to sleep.

WEDNESDAY

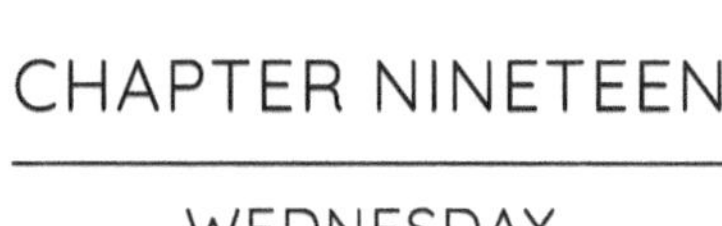

I SLEPT like shit last night. Actually, that's not true. I slept hard for the first half of the night after Devon owned my body. I'm not sure if it was more fun being a bad girl or a good girl. Unfortunately, when I woke up to pee at 2:45, it was all downhill from there. My brain took over, and I was in a fit of restless sleep over this interview.

This interview that I was awake at 4:30 in the morning for, so I can get to the airport on time for my 6:30 flight to New York. I'm a little queasy from being up so early, though Devon managed to make a decent breakfast sandwich for me and a latte, so I have something to eat on the way to the airport.

"I wish you'd let me take you," he whispers, holding me close in the house's entryway. My ride pulls up outside, and my heart constricts at having to say goodbye to him. These last few years apart have sucked. I cried every time we said goodbye, and that was just as friends—even if I was in love with him but hadn't admitted it. I reason with myself, reminding my achy heart that I'll be back tomorrow night.

He hugs me tighter, and this is why I won't let him take me. I won't get on the plane if he does. We're still in the just-got-together honeymoon period. The last thing I want is to say goodbye to him, and no doubt my heart would take over if I tried at the airport.

"You have plenty to do at the inn, plus I don't want you driving when you're tired. Anyway, I'll be back tomorrow. It'll barely be thirty-six hours apart," I say as much for me as for him.

He sighs, twisting his fingers through the strands of hair that have fallen out of my messy ponytail. "And I'll be there waiting when you get off the plane." He kisses the side of my head. "You're going to kick ass, babe."

"Assuming I'm not too jet-lagged to function."

He steps back and squints at me. "You'll do amazing. Come on."

He picks up my bag—just a small carry on since I have clothes back at my apartment—and opens the front door. Reluctantly, I follow him out.

At the car, he puts my bag in the backseat, then presses me against the back of the car and kisses me again. "Call me tonight and I'll see you tomorrow." There's a look of deep longing in his eyes that matches the feeling in my soul. "Love you."

"Love you too. I'll text you when I get there."

After one last kiss and a lingering look, I climb into the car. He shuts the door behind me, but I immediately roll down the window.

"Fly safe," he says, stepping back from the car.

"I'll do my best." As I wave, the car pulls away, and I feel the same emptiness I always feel when I say goodbye to him. Thankfully, the reminder I keep giving myself that I'll be back soon is keeping me from bawling like I usually do.

With a deep breath, I open my foil-wrapped sandwich and munch on it while focusing on what's ahead of me. It'll feel good to walk into that office with my head held high. My former department head was a pig who got what was coming to him, and I'm returning triumphant, like a scene from a movie. As a senior editor, I'd be overseeing other staff and helping them with their pieces. And I might finally get the chance to do more human-interest pieces between reviewing books. It's my dream job.

At least, that's what my dream job would be if I wrote down a bullet point list. Not to mention finally feeling like I made it. That was always part of the plan. Get my foot in the door and work my way up. Have a strong career doing the thing I love—writing.

I thought all that was taken from me. Now I have a path back. Yet something feels off. Not to return to old analogies, but it feels like someone left the door open, and I'm wandering through. *Seems like a good option. Might as well take it.*

If I do take it, what does that mean for Devon and me? He said we'd figure it out together, that he'd be with me anywhere, but would he really just pack up and leave his life behind for me to take this job? Would it be fair for me to ask that of him?

I don't know.

But it wouldn't have to be forever. I could use this job to gain experience, then find something based in San Francisco. We could move back here. Until then we could visit often. The benefit of being a writer is that you can write from anywhere. I could write at the inn, or even the library, so I wouldn't have to completely give those things up.

Why hasn't any of this excited me?

Writing is what I want to do, right?

"Would you like to listen to anything?" the driver asks, snapping me out of my thoughts.

I glance up at the rearview, then down at the phone in my hand. "No. That's all right, thanks. I've got something to listen to on my phone."

He nods, and I slip my earbuds in, pulling up one of my favorite audiobooks.

Can't quiet your brain? Nothing like listening to a fictional character's problems instead.

WHEN WE PULL up at the drop off section of San Francisco International Airport, I'm not feeling any more confident than I was on the ride here. Instead of my audiobook distracting me, my brain kept twisting over whether writing is my dream. If I'm chasing it or running away from my own happiness.

Absolutely none of that is this driver's problem, though, and he's been great, so I hand him a cash tip—that way I know no one else is taking a cut of it—grab my bag, and climb out.

Standing in front of the massive building, my brain only speeds up, the sickening feeling in my stomach growing.

I don't want to get on this plane.

But why not?

It's the dream job, I tell myself for the thousandth time. And then I hear a tiny voice inside of me. A ghost from the past. *How is it possibly the dream if you have to leave your family behind?* I thought those words when we moved here from New York. Granted, that move worked for me. I found something in Brighton. Maybe I found it all over again when I came back. I found a home I didn't know I'd been looking for. Not because of Devon—though he's a part of it. He always has been. Something about this place, this community, it feels like home to me. And it's where I want to be.

I love my cousins, my parents, and my friends in New York, but even if Devon came with me, I know I wouldn't be as happy there as I am here.

That's it. Decision made.

I'm staying.

My heart lightens the second the words move through my

brain. A weight lifts, and the feeling of freedom and peace I've had since I got back to Brighton returns.

Looking down at my phone, I open the app to call for another car to take me back to Brighton, but when I spin around, I see Chris, Brighton's number one cabbie, leaning against the side of his van. He grins at me.

I tuck my phone away and hurry over to him.

"Part of me wants to question if you're some sort of supernatural being who appears whenever someone needs you, but the rest of me just needs to know if you're heading back to Brighton."

"I am," he says. "To your other question, I just dropped someone off. Then I saw you standing here and recognized you from the other day. I thought I'd wait and see if you needed a ride before I took off."

"Thank you," I sigh. "You are the best cab driver ever."

He smiles proudly. "That's the goal. Hopefully, one day, I'll have a better van than this."

I laugh to myself at the wood paneled blue van that screams childhood memories. Everyone either had or knew someone who had a van like this. It reminds me of every early 2000s TV show I've ever watched.

"The van is epic," I tell him.

"Glad you feel that way. Shall we?"

"Absolutely. I'm ready to go home."

CHAPTER TWENTY

Devon

KENNEDY LEAVING PUT me in an immediate funk. It shouldn't be bothering me this much. She's coming back tomorrow. I won't even have to go thirty-six hours without her.

"Here," Justin says, sliding a latte in front of me. "Drink. You look like someone kicked your puppy."

"I don't have a puppy."

"You know what I mean," he says, dropping onto a nearby stool as I stare at the mug in front of me. "Do you want to talk about it?"

I shrug. "It's fine."

"It's obviously not. You look like you're about to start crying into your latte. I thought you wanted her to take the interview."

"I do."

He blinks at me. "But you also don't?"

I clear my throat. "I don't want to hold her back from her dreams. I'm so fucking proud of her. She worked so many shitty jobs to get to this point. This is her dream. Why should I take that from her just because I don't want to go to New York?"

I wince as the words leave my mouth. In turn, Justin's eyes widen.

"Wow. Have you told Kend that?"

My lips pull into a flat line. "No. Because it's not just about me."

"Right, it's about both of you. Your opinion matters, too. Why don't you want to go to New York?"

"I—" my phone goes off before I can answer. Seeing my mother's name, I quickly swipe it off the counter and answer. "Hi, Mom. What's up?"

"Devon, honey," her voice is urgent, and I immediately stand up, heart racing. "Your dad had a fall."

"How bad?" I ask, hurrying toward the front door. Concerned, Justin hops off his stool and follows me.

"Not sure yet. He lost consciousness for a minute, but he's awake now. The ambulance is here, but you know the drill. They won't let me ride with them."

"I'm leaving now. I'll be there as fast as I can."

"Don't drive like an idiot. I love you."

"Love you too, Mom."

"What happened?" Justin asks as I grab my keys and dash out the door, sprinting down the walk to my 4Runner.

"Dad fell. I need to get my mom so we can meet the ambulance at the hospital," I call behind me as I jump into the driver's seat.

Justin runs around the front and hops in the passenger side. "Okay. Do you need me to call anyone? Kennedy?"

I hand him my phone as I start the car and back out of the driveway.

"I'll call her later. Just let me know if my mom calls or texts."

Justin side-eyes me but doesn't argue.

Maybe I should call Kennedy, but she's probably already boarding her flight. There's nothing she can do. I'd rather not upset her before her interview. I want her to kick ass, even if I've realized I really like the life I've built here, far more than I liked living in New York.

Fuck, this is too much right now.

My phone goes off, and I look over at Justin, who is reading a text.

"Your mom said Gladys was close and picked her up. They're headed to the hospital and want you to meet them there."

I shift in the seat, not moving my gaze from the windshield. "Okay."

Taking the turn for the hospital, I focus only on getting there quickly. Thankfully, since it's a Wednesday morning, there isn't much traffic.

I'm rigid in my seat as I stare at the empty road in front of me. I shouldn't be this worked up. It's not the first fall my dad has had. It won't be his last. Maybe that's the most upsetting thing. There's nothing I can do to help him. To slow the progression of this disease. I didn't expect it to take so much of him so quickly. This is just one fall, but all too often, one fall leads to another and another and he's in a flare-up, or worse, another downslide.

As I pull into the parking lot, my stomach churns. I wish Kennedy were here with me. I've gone through this alone for years. I have my mother, Gladys, and many wonderful folks around town who help and support us, but emotionally, I've gone through it all alone.

It's your own fault she's not here.

I wanted her to take the interview. She's worked too hard to let it pass by, but what if she gets this job? Will it be more long hours where I barely see her? Or worse, if something like this happens, will I have to fly back alone because she can't leave her job? Now I feel like an asshole again for even thinking that. She deserves to have everything she wants in her life.

Pulling into a spot, I let out a long breath and clench my hand around the steering wheel as I shut off the car.

Justin looks over at me when I don't open my door.

"You need a minute?"

I stare at him for a second, then shake my head. "No. Let's go."

We get out of the car and head inside. Not seeing my mom or Gladys, I send Gladys a text in case Mom is busy with Dad or a doctor.

> Just got here. Where are you?

GLADYS

> Oh good. There're double doors at the edge of the ER. We're down a hall in another waiting room. Let the staff know who you're here for and they should let you through.

> Thanks.

I gesture for Justin to follow me, and go to the check-in desk, letting them know who we're here for. They let us through the double doors, and we quickly find the waiting room.

"Mom," I call, hurrying over and pulling her into my arms.

"It's all right, dear," she says softly.

When I let her go, I take her hands. "What happened?"

She sighs. "He wanted a breakfast sandwich, and he didn't want me to get up and make it for him. Thankfully, he let me sit in my chair in the kitchen and hand him things. He was turning to pick something up from the table when he lost his footing, fell backward, and caught his head on the edge of the counter."

My eyes go wide. "Jesus, Mom. That doesn't sound like it's all right. Where is he now?"

"Getting a CT and an MRI. He was conscious and making jokes with the ambulance crew when they left, so I think he'll be fine."

"This time. What about next time? I know you—and especially Dad—don't want to rely on me or an aide, but you need to. This could've been worse. What if he'd been in there alone? We have to come up with a better plan."

Mom nods solemnly. "I suppose we do."

"I'm sorry. I'm not trying to take your independence. That's the last thing I want, but I need you to be safe."

"I know, sweetheart. Once this is all settled with your dad, we'll talk about it, okay?"

"Yeah. Okay."

She looks around, then waves at Justin. "Where's Kennedy?"

"She had to fly back to New York this morning."

"Oh, that's right. I hope it all goes well for her. Did you call her?"

"Not yet."

She furrows her brow. "Why not?"

"She's on the plane. Nothing she can do."

Mom shakes her head. "There are other ways to reach her." When I don't say anything, she sighs. "Hopefully the doctor will be out soon. Try not to worry."

"Sure."

I help her back into her chair next to Gladys, then take a seat in a row of chairs across from her next to Justin.

"You okay?" he asks.

"I guess. Just worried."

"Your dad's tough. He'll be okay." He's quiet for a second, then asks, "Do you want me to message Kennedy? She can't answer her phone, but she'll have Wi-Fi access, at least."

"No, that's okay. There's nothing she can do on the plane, anyway."

"And so she doesn't deserve to know? To be able to support you?"

"How is she going to support me from there?"

He squints at me. "Are you pissed she left? Because you've been encouraging her to go."

"I'm not pissed that she left. I would never want to stand in the way of her dreams."

His brows pinch together. "But you want to stay in Brighton?" I nod slowly. "Because of your parents? Because you know there's nothing *you* could've done, right? You being here can't change or prevent things like this from happening. Don't use this as your excuse not to leave."

"I know," I huff. "Believe me, I know. I wish I could change it, but I can't. Of course I want to be here to support my parents in moments like this, but that's not why I don't want to leave. Until recently, I thought it was, but I think I was using it as an excuse. I'm actually... happy here. I didn't think I would be. That probably doesn't make any sense since I grew up here."

"No," he says gently, "I get it. I left New York to move home first, remember? Thing is, I feel more at home there than I did in Chicago or Manhattan, but I still feel like I'm trying to find my place. Or maybe the right person. I don't know. If you feel at home here, that's a big thing. I get it."

"I never thought I'd end up feeling like this. Like this is where I want to build my future. The only thing that's been missing is Kennedy."

"I'm guessing you haven't told her this?"

"No."

"Why not?"

"Because her career is important."

"And what you want isn't?" He stares at me for a moment, like he's figuring out some complex math problem.

"What?" I grit out.

"I'm trying to figure out if you've always been like this, or if it started when you moved back here."

"Been like what?"

"Someone who sacrifices their wants and needs for everyone else."

I scoff. "That's not what I do."

"Let's check the score. How many years did you put your feelings for Kennedy away simply because you didn't want to push her? When your parents called and asked for help, you didn't fly home for a few weeks, you packed all your shit and moved to the opposite side of the country even though you'd just gotten a killer new job. And now, when you're settled and enjoying life in Brighton, you're going to pack up and move to the other side of the country *again* without a second thought if Kennedy gets this job. Scoreboard says: self-sacrifice."

Fuck him for being right.

But he's not done. "Jesus, that's the same reason you aren't calling Kennedy now, isn't it? Man, you're an idiot."

"Thanks for that."

"I'm serious. You're trying to protect Kennedy, not upset her, let her have this job—whatever. Have you ever stopped and thought that she deserves to know what happened with your dad this morning? Because she cares about your parents. She cares about you. Do you think it would make her happy to know you'd move across the country even though you don't want to? That's not how real, healthy relationships work."

"I don't want to ruin things. Yes, we've loved each other for a long time, but we only just got together. This is a big thing."

"Right. So, talking about it is absolutely *not* the answer." He rolls his eyes and shakes his head. "I've narrated enough romances to know that not talking about shit is a much faster way to ruin things than talking about the hard stuff. You and Kennedy have a strong relationship because it's rooted in your friendship. She deserves to know how you feel and you deserve to have what you want in life, too. And I promise you, taking all choices away from her by just going along with things and not telling her the truth is not how you're going to get that."

I stare at him, frustration and anger rumbling in my stomach. I wish I could be mad at him, but damn it, he's so fucking right it hurts.

"I'll talk to her," I say finally.

"Wow, you act like you're taking a knife to the gut."

Pushing out a breath, I say. "I love her. I love her so fucking much it doesn't make sense. I didn't know how deeply I could love until we finally opened our hearts to each other. The last thing I want is for her to feel like she has to choose between a job and me. But you're right. I shouldn't keep things from her. As soon as we talk to the doctor, I'll send her a message and tell her what happened."

"Good."

Until then, I'll keep being a massive chicken shit.

Solid plan.

CHAPTER TWENTY-ONE

Kennedy

THE ENTIRE RIDE back to Brighton, my mind was ablaze, but this time in the best way, as I figured out what I'd need to do to stay in Brighton permanently. That word is still a little scary, but in an exciting way.

The top three things on the list were:

- *Pack my apartment and ship my things out here.*
- *Get a car and probably a California driver's license.*
- *Figure out a job.*

Then I realized I don't need to figure out a job. I already have plenty to do in Brighton. And I love it all. I get to be a part of this community and bring people together.

That's when Gladys's words hit me all over again. *"It's not about what you do, it's about who you are."*

I was so focused on having a career that I never stopped to

think about whether I enjoyed it. I suppose on some level I did, but I wasn't nearly as happy as I've been being a part of this community. I love writing, yes. But what I love more is what I use writing for—to connect with people. Something that's always come naturally, that's important to me. That's who I am. And it's what I want to do.

While I'll never stop writing, I decided I'm going to return to freelance work—writing the stories *I* want to write. The ones that mean the most. Then I'll balance the rest of my time between working at the inn, volunteering at the library, and occasionally helping Claire.

That's when I found myself tearing up in the back of Chris's van and trying not to be obvious over the fact that I was crying.

My mother's words flashed through my mind again. *It's always the last key that opens the door.* I finally found the right key, and it turns out I had it all along. I just needed to know where to look.

I considered going straight to the inn and jumping into Devon's arms, but opted to have Chris drop me off at the house instead so I could set up a surprise for Devon. When we got here, Devon's car was gone, and so were both of the boys. Justin must've gone with Devon to the inn, which is a plus for me, because I can get him to persuade Devon to come back here early.

I wipe some sweat off my brow as I step in the back door. I just finished setting up the tent in the backyard, which was more physical labor than I remembered. Probably because Devon usually set the tent up. But I'm determined to surprise him. I want him to know this is what I want more than anything. This is where I want to be. Building a life here with him.

After grabbing a glass of water, I check my phone, which I left sitting on the kitchen counter, and see texts from Justin and Gladys.

JUSTIN

Hey, so Devon is being a stubborn moron and not messaging you, but I thought you should know his dad fell. It's not horrible, but we're all at the hospital. Maybe message or call him when you can.

I'm already locking the back door as I check the text from Gladys.

GLADYS

Hi honey, hope your flight is going well. Listen, Lon fell this morning. He's doing okay, but Devon is upset. I'm not sure why he hasn't called you yet, but I think he needs to talk to you. I think hearing your voice would do him good, if there's any way you can swing it.
Love you.

Shit! But also, *why didn't he call me?*

Whatever. It doesn't matter. He needs me right now, and the rest of it can be sorted out later.

Spinning around, I dash toward the front of the house, unbelievably thankful to find the keys to Justin's rental car on the hook by the door. Grabbing my purse and the keys, I quickly head outside, locking the door behind me as I go.

I need to get to Devon. That's the only thing on my mind as I drive to the hospital. That and I hope his dad is okay. It didn't sound horrible, but it sounds like Devon is taking it hard. I wouldn't know since he didn't call me. Of course, he thought I was on the plane, but still. Not even a message?

Now I'm even more grateful I didn't get on that flight. I don't ever want him to have to go through things like this alone. That's why he has me. I hate that we wasted so much time getting together, but now that we are, I'm never letting him face the hard things in life alone ever again.

I park near Devon's car and head in through the emergency room entrance. The woman at the check-in desk tells me the family is in a nearby waiting room and ushers me through a set of locked double doors.

When I find the waiting area, Devon is sitting next to Justin across from his mom and Gladys.

Gladys looks up and sees me first, shooting me a wink. Then she elbows Sharon, who looks at me and smiles. Off their looks, Justin turns and looks at me, smiling knowingly. Devon, who is still engrossed in his phone, hasn't looked up. Quietly, I walk over and sit down next to him.

"Couldn't even message me, huh?"

He spins to face me with wide eyes, sputtering for words. "What are you doing here? Shouldn't you be on the plane?"

I shrug and smile. "Found a parachute."

"Kend..."

"I—"

"Is this the family of Lon McGregor?"

We all turn toward a doctor who has stepped into the room.

"That's us," Sharon says, gripping the edges of her chair and pushing herself up to stand as Devon stands, ready to jump in and help her.

I stand too and take his hand. I have so much respect for the way he gives his mother space even when it's hard for him. He wants to help and protect her, but she wants to hold on to her independence. It takes strength to recognize how to help someone and both be there but not overstep. I squeeze his hand harder as I realize just how much of a toll all this has taken on him. He hid it well, and I wish he wouldn't have. Being a caregiver is hard. When my grandmother was at the end of her life, my mom and my aunt took care of her nonstop. They refused to hire an aide, switching off time with her. It took so much out of them. Devon isn't even thirty, and he's doing it for both of his parents. He deserves to have someone to take care of him. Even if he's not particularly good at letting anyone do that. I'm just going to have to force it on him.

"Your husband is doing well overall. We're going to keep him overnight for observation. We did both a CT of his head and an MRI. The CT showed no trauma, and we'll have the MRI results back in a day or two. The MRI will indicate if he's having a flare-up, so we can be prepared."

"Okay, thank you, doctor. When can I get back to see him?"

"They're in the process of getting him a bed for the night. For now, you can come back to his room in the ER. Just one at a time."

Devon nods at his mom, and she slowly follows the doctor down the hall. Once she's out of sight, his gaze turns back to me.

"Seriously, Kend, what are you doing here?"

I put my free hand on my hip and narrow my eyes at him. "We can talk about that after you tell me why you didn't call or message me."

He stares at me for a second, then sighs. "Come on. Let's find somewhere private."

I nod, and though I'm feeling more than a little frustrated with him right now, I don't let go of his hand.

We end up in the backseat of his 4Runner.

"I'm sorry," he says after a moment. "I should have talked to you as soon as I heard about my dad. I didn't want to worry you before your interview."

"This is more important. Things like this will *always* be more important," I say, hand still wrapped around his. I'm mad, but we're in this together. Whatever it is.

"Why didn't you get on the plane?" he asks softly.

"Because I didn't want to. I stood in front of the airport and felt like I was leaving my home—the life I really wanted."

His eyes widen. "Really?"

"Yes. In the last week and a half, I've been happier than I have been in a long time. I enjoyed my life in New York, but I wasn't happy like I am here. Brighton feels like home. It's where I want to build a life. With you."

"But not just because I'm here, right? Because I don't want you to stay just for me."

I tilt my head as I take him in. "No. I just told you, it's everything. You are a part of that happiness, not all of it."

He lets out a long breath. "Okay, good. This is where I want to be, too."

Well, he could've told me that.

I probably would've come to my own conclusion about that a lot sooner if he hadn't been so pushy about me going.

He leans forward and wraps his arms around me, but I give him a little shove backward. His brow furrows in confusion as he looks at me.

"Devon, what would you have said if I had wanted to go back to New York?"

He gives a little shrug. "I'd have gone with you. I just want you to be happy."

I grab his hands and squeeze them tightly. "Let me make one thing very clear, I'm never going to be happy if you're sacrificing yourself and not communicating with me. I know we didn't admit our feelings for a long time, but otherwise, we've always been open and honest with each other…" I trail off. "Or at least I have. You haven't been honest with me when you've needed help or support. That has to stop. I respect what you've done for your parents. You're a good man and a great son, but hiding your feelings and never asking for help stops right now. You don't have to handle anything alone anymore. You've got me. Lean on me. I'm here for you. Every step. I promise."

"I'm sorry. I love you. Can I kiss you now?"

"Only if you promise to share your feelings and needs with me from now on. And no more blind sacrificing."

"I promise." He leans in and softly kisses my lips, increasing the pressure and drawing me closer with every movement of his lips.

When he pulls away, he asks, "What about the job, Kend? It's what you've been working for."

"It was," I say softly. "But over the last week and a half, I've realized it's not what I want after all. I want to do something I enjoy every day. And that's what working at the inn and volunteering at the library, and even helping Claire, have given me. I'll never stop writing, but now I'm going to switch back to freelance and write what I want to write."

"As long as you're happy—"

"As long as we're both happy."

"You're staying, I have a job I enjoy, a great community, and a home I love. I'm happy."

"Yeah? Does that mean you want me to live with you?"

"Fuck yes. Where else would you live?"

"I'm assuming there are apartments in Brighton."

"There are. But you aren't living in them. I already told you, I dreamed of having you stay with me. There's no way I'm letting you live anywhere else." He leans in and kisses me. "You're staying right here." Another kiss. "With me." One more kiss. "I love you."

I loop my arms around his neck and lean into him. "I love you too." Then I trace my tongue over his bottom lip before pushing it into his mouth and deepening our kiss. I can't believe I waited so damn long to go for it with him. I knew it would be a risk, and that scared me off, but I never factored in the rewards. Falling for your best friend is scary as hell, but when it works, it really works.

I sigh against his lips and pull away, resting my forehead against his and looking into his eyes.

"We should probably go back inside."

"Yeah, probably. I need to be sure my mom eats something."

I kiss him again before he can move. "Remember, we're in it together."

He grabs my hand and kisses it. "I know. Thank you. We better get out of the car now or we never will."

I laugh at that and swing my door open.

As we walk back to the hospital hand in hand, Devon says, "So, I know you're still figuring out the specifics of job stuff, but if you're interested, Gladys and I have been talking for months about creating a new part time position at the inn."

"Doing what?"

"Event planning. We have weddings there throughout the year, and they've steadily increased since I've been back. People often ask if we have an on-site event planner or even someone their planner can coordinate with. Gladys helps with coordinating, but I think you'd be incredible at it. You're great at putting people at ease, listening, and getting to the heart of what they need. I know it would be a career pivot, so I don't want an answer right away. Take some time and think about it."

"I'm definitely interested. Maybe I could try it out for a little while and see how it goes."

"That sounds perfect. That way you can figure out how much of your time you want to spend on each thing."

"It's funny, I was so focused on having a specific career, I didn't realize how much I could enjoy myself by doing what comes naturally to me, and following my heart."

"And that's what you're doing now?"

"Absolutely. And building a life here, with you, makes me more excited than I've been in a long time."

"Good answer," he says with a quick kiss, then together, we walk inside.

CHAPTER TWENTY-TWO

Devon

AFTER A LONG DAY spent at the hospital, crappy sandwiches from the cafeteria, and an ill-fated attempt to get my mother to sleep at home instead of the awful sleeper sofa in Dad's room, I finally turn onto Apple Lane and head toward my house. My fingers are intertwined with Kennedy's as our arms rest on the center console. *Our* house.

I still feel like a jackass for not talking to her, but that's a lesson learned. It's weird starting a relationship with someone you've known for most of your life. There's a learning curve to the relationship, but we already know each other so well. In most ways, it's like we're jumping into the middle of a serious relationship, but we're still learning how to communicate and actually be in a relationship. Not that any of that is bad, but it requires a tremendous amount of grace and forgiveness and communication. Thankfully, Kennedy has all that in spades, and I'm remembering how to open up and let someone else in. It meant a lot to have her by my side today. To feel like I had a partner.

In her, I know I do.

As I pull into the driveway and put the car in park, I let out a deep breath. As I shut the car off, I look through the windshield, squinting when I see something in the backyard.

A tent.

"Kend, what's that?"

"Huh?" She follows my gaze. "Oh! With everything that happened, I forgot. I came straight here from the airport and started setting up a surprise." She gives me a sheepish smile, and I grab her arm, pulling her to me and kissing her deeply.

"It's perfect. I can't wait to camp with you tonight. And maybe... a few other things."

She laughs as I kiss her again, then we finally get out of the car.

"Oh good, you two finally decided to stop making out. I thought I was going to have to break into the house," Justin says, leaning against his rental car.

"Sorry, not sorry," Kennedy says with a grin, strolling past me toward the house and pulling out her keys.

Once inside, we head for the kitchen. It must be almost dinner time, but I'm not particularly hungry. Seeing marshmallows and hot chocolate packets on the counter, though, I smile.

"Saw the tent out back. Does that mean we're finally having our camp out?" Justin asks.

Kennedy and I both spin to face him.

"I..." I begin, as Kennedy says, "Well..."

Justin stares at us for a beat, then laughs out loud. "Hah. You should see your faces. Don't worry. I have no intention of joining you. But someday, the three of us are going camping together for real."

"That would be fun," Kennedy says. "Maybe for our bachelor and bachelorette parties." Her cheeks go pink and she stumbles over her words. "You know, whenever we get that far."

A pleased smile grows on my face as I step over and wrap my

arms around her waist, rumbling in her ear, "Whenever we get there."

Justin laughs dryly. "Yeah, I have no desire to be around the two of you tonight, so have fun. Happy boning."

Kennedy reaches over and smacks him as he walks out of the room.

"You act like that's not what we're going to be doing." I kiss down her neck, giving her a chill, but she just smiles coyly.

"I have no idea why you'd think we'd be doing *that.*"

She tries to step back, but I pull her closer. "Mm, remember how I said I wanted to fuck you on the counter?"

"You *did* fuck me on the counter."

"Well, yes. But that wasn't the ultimate fantasy. That was always the two of us alone in the tent, and there would be some moment where we'd attack each other. In fact," I drag my finger down her chest to the cleavage that's showing. "I used to imagine I'd lose my virginity to you like that."

Heat swells in her eyes as she looks at me. Then she kisses my cheek and pushes out of my arms. "Guess you should've made your move, then."

She turns toward the counter, gathering all the campfire supplies.

Wrapping my arms around her waist, I graze my lips below her ear and whisper, "What do you think I'm doing right now?" She sucks in a ragged breath, and I move to her other side, doing the same thing below her other ear. "And I'm just getting started." Then I stand up straight and step back. "I'm going to get changed. Meet you out there."

I walk out of the room, smiling to myself.

I love teasing my girl.

I DROP the wood I found for the fire next to the firepit, then slide off my sandals and climb into the tent. I've just gotten comfortable when the tent unzips and Kennedy appears. I choke on a breath as I stare at her.

Jesus damn.

"Kennedy, are those the sleep shorts?"

She looks at me innocently as she sits down next to me. "Which shorts?"

My eyes flare and I run my hand up her leg. "The ones from when you were a teenager?"

She looks down in mock surprise. "Huh. What do you know? I guess they are."

I shake my head, then tackle her, pinning her beneath me as she giggles. I run my hands up her arms, holding them above her head as I dip my head down, kissing down her neck and across her collarbone as I rock my pelvis against her.

"Devon?" she mumbles.

"Hm?"

"Is that the same boner? From when you were a teenager?" She cocks an eyebrow and smirks.

"For you? Always." Then I sink my teeth into her neck as she moans.

"Devon," she breathes, "we have to be quiet. What if our parents hear?"

It takes a second for me to realize what she's doing.

"I don't know if I can be quiet. I want you so bad, Kennedy."

"I can't believe I'm losing my virginity to you."

"You want this, right? Us?"

"You know I do." She tugs my sweats and boxers down, then fists my cock.

"If you touch me like that, I won't last long." I wish I could say that's me pretending, but I'm not. Her hand on me sets me off, the warmth of her skin sending a tingle down my spine.

"We can't have that," she says. "I need to know what it feels like with you inside me."

"What if I come right away?" I ask, playing around this time.

"We'll just have to do it again. And again. And again. Until we have it perfect."

"That we will," I say, sliding those sinful shorts down along with her panties. "We've got all night."

"We've got even longer than that," Kennedy says, looking into my eyes as I thrust into her. "We've got a lifetime."

I bury myself inside her, my hot lips on hers, and lose myself in everything we are together and the future we're going to have.

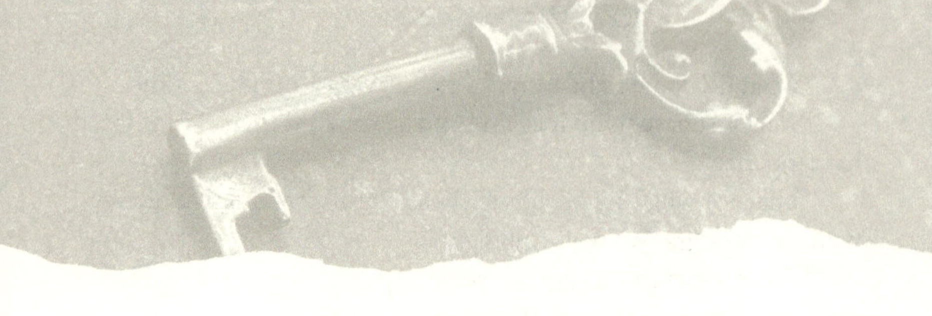

CHAPTER TWENTY-THREE

FRIDAY

Kennedy

I'M TYPING AWAY on my phone as Devon drives us to the reunion meet and greet at the high school. Tomorrow is the actual reunion at the inn. Ever since I made the decision to stay in Brighton, it's been a whirlwind of telling people and planning when to go back to New York to pack my stuff. Though I'll ship some of it, other things I want right away, since when I packed for Brighton, I didn't factor in more than a couple of weeks worth of clothes.

I also want to see my parents and Hallie. Though my mom was a little sad I was leaving *and* giving up on my "career," she was overall supportive and glad to see me happy. Hallie was also happy for me, but like Devon, I know she won't tell me the full truth, then she'll deal with it alone. Leaving her alone is the only hard thing about moving here. We've lived together for the past few years, and we've grown even closer since Frannie moved to Ida. Thankfully, I won't be leaving her in the lurch with rent since our parents own the small three-story building. But I will miss sharing an apartment with her, and I hope she'll be okay on her own.

Eventually, I hope she'll find the right person. Someone who will force her to let them take care of her. That's what she needs, whether she'd ever admit it or not.

"Okay, does next Friday sound good for going back to New York to grab my stuff?" I ask Devon. "Hallie says Frannie and Mark will be there for a long weekend too."

"Justin's heading there on Thursday. We should go then too, so we can all have a few days together." He squeezes my hand, which has been intertwined with his since we left the house.

"And you're sure that's what *you* want?"

He smiles, then lifts my hand to his lips and kisses it. "Positive."

"Good. Because flights are not cheap." I grimace at my phone, then a text pops up from Hallie.

> **HALLIE**
> Don't worry, I started packing for you.

> What? No.

> **HALLIE**
> Yes. By the way, who keeps their vibrators in their underwear drawer anymore? You have a bedside table.

I squeak in disbelief.

"What?" Devon asks.

"Nothing."

He pulls into the parking lot as I furiously text Hallie back.

> Stop immediately!

> **HALLIE**
> Why? I've already seen the naughty bits.
> Besides, I have one of the same ones.

Wait. Which one?

HALLIE

The duckie one.

Shut up. But it's amazing, right?

HALLIE

The question is, is it better than Devon?

"Oh, I definitely need to know the answer to that," Devon says over my shoulder, scaring the shit out of me. I hadn't even realized he'd pulled into a parking space.

I quickly click my phone screen off and turn to face him.

"Hm. I'm not sure."

His eyes darken and he leans in, pushing me back against my seat. "You're not sure?" He drags his nose up the side of my neck then quickly sucks the skin between his lips. A whimper escapes before I can stop myself. He pulls back, grinning evilly. "Don't you remember what happens to bad girls?"

"Maybe I like being bad."

His facade cracks and he groans. "Damn it, Kend. I can't go in there with a boner."

"You started it."

He takes a big breath in and lets it out. "I love you. Even when you give me blue balls."

I laugh at that. "Well, you've given me lady blue balls plenty of times over the years. Still, if there's somewhere you want to sneak off to…"

"You're going to kill me."

He plants a steamy kiss on my lips, pulling away tantalizingly slowly. "We should get in there." Then he swings his door open. God, he's such a clit tease.

A moment later, he appears at my door and opens it for me, extending his hand like he's the prince taking the princess to the ball. And just like that my horniness is replaced by swooning. Mostly.

"So, plane tickets are bad, huh?"

"Not the worst ever, but they're not great."

"Good thing I've done nothing but save for the last three years. It'll be fine."

We walk hand in hand to the entrance of the school. As soon as we walk in, there's a table for us to sign in. We get our name badges, which we'll need for tomorrow night as well. The meet and greet tonight is being held in the gym, so we head there, finding tables set up around the perimeter with pictures all over them.

Hands intertwined, we walk around the gym, stopping to chat with former classmates here and there. More than a few point out how unsurprising it is that we're a couple. Were we really that blind to each other's feelings?

"Hey," Devon says, pointing to a picture of the two of us.

We stop, and I pick it up, getting the answer to my question.

Yep, we were very blind.

In the picture, we're standing, facing each other, leaning against the lockers as we talk. His head is tipped down toward me, and I'm looking up at him. If I didn't know any better, I'd think we were a couple in that picture. He looks like he's about to kiss me, and I look like a giggly girl in love.

Maybe I always was.

"Did you ever think we'd end up together?" I ask him. In a complete fantasy sense, I dreamed we would, but I never let myself believe it.

"Come with me," he says, leading me out of the gym and over to the lockers. He searches for a minute until he finds mine. "Do you remember Troy?"

I snort at the mention of his name. "Uh, yeah. I think I remember my douchey boyfriend from junior year who broke up with me because he needed to focus on football. Even though football season was over. I didn't realize at the time how awful he was, and I was heartbroken."

He nods slowly. "You stood there against your locker trying not to cry."

"I hate crying in public."

"I know. And I knew all you wanted to do was fall apart, so rather than hug you—which I knew would make you sob—I listened to and encouraged your rant about him. Unfortunately, it eventually veered into hysterical territory and you went off on a tangent about how you must be unlovable and you'd end up alone and would probably be the only single person at our high school reunion."

My eyes grow wider as I remember the moment. "And you told me that would never be the case. I was too amazing to end up alone. Then you told me that worst case, we'd go to the reunion together and pretend to be a couple." Looking into his eyes, I softly shake my head. "Did you think it would be for real?"

"I hoped it would be." He tucks a strand of hair behind my ear and looks down into my eyes, just like he was in that picture. "Most of the time, that felt like a longshot. But for that moment, it felt like a possibility. A part of me held onto it. Now here we are."

"Here we are," I breathe. Pressing onto my toes, I wrap my hand around the back of his neck and crush my lips against his in a sloppy, passionate kiss. He pulls me closer, his hands on my ass as his tongue tangles with mine. At the sound of clattering in the hallway, he pulls away, softly kissing my lips one more time as I sigh. "Isn't there a room around here where people used to go to have sex?"

He chuckles, resting his forehead against mine. "How about we just go home? We'll have all of tomorrow to hang out with everyone."

A smile grows on my face as warmth spreads through me.

"What?" he asks.

"*Home.* I love that it's my home now, too."

"And it always will be." He squeezes my hand, then kisses my cheek before leading me out of the school.

CHAPTER TWENTY-FOUR

SATURDAY

THE BALLROOM of the inn is a ghost of dances past. There are streamers everywhere in our school colors—red and gold—with the same colored balloons as the centerpiece for each table. It throws me right back to high school dances, many of which were spent with the gorgeous girl next to me.

"Oh my gosh," Kennedy says with something between a gasp and a laugh. "Quite the transformation from yesterday morning."

"It definitely is."

"Oh, look," she says, pointing toward the projector screen where photos of us from high school next to current ones flash over the screen. She watches for a moment until hers appear. "Thanks for picking a good picture of me. You could have told me I needed to give them one."

"You could have checked the email. I just assumed you didn't, since you didn't mention it. And I don't have any bad pictures of you."

She spins to face me, eyebrows raised. "We both know that's a lie. Do you not remember all those selfies we used to take?"

I bite my lip and pull out my phone, unlocking it and showing her the background. "You mean like this one?"

Her eyes flare. "Really? Of all the pictures of us, *that* is your home screen?"

The picture is from when we lived in New York. We're at her apartment, and for some reason she's licking my face. Based on the look in our eyes, we're both pretty drunk, and I'd bet money we cuddled in bed that night while both dreaming we'd take things further.

"It was the closest I got to kissing you."

"Well, we need to change that. Come here."

She leads me over to the wall, standing in front of a Brighton High Bison's poster. Grabbing my phone, she holds it up and snaps a selfie of her kissing my cheek. When she's done, I snatch the phone from her hand and hold it out, then pull her close and capture her lips in a soft kiss as I snap a picture.

"Perfect," I say, looking at them and setting the one I took as my home screen and the one she took as my lock screen.

"Wow," she says, looking around the room again. "This takes me back. Prom. Homecoming. All those high school dances." She tilts her head as she looks up at me. "Dances we always seemed to go to together. Was that a coincidence?"

I smile wide. "Nope. If we went to dances together, I had an excuse to hold you, dance with you, spend the evening with you. In my mind, it became a tradition after I asked you to homecoming freshman year. I tried to always be single for homecoming, and when it came time, I was determined to take you to prom."

"Which you did," she says softly.

"You wore that silver and dark gray dress. Smokey eyes—"

"Courtesy of Claire."

"And your hair was long and relaxed. Your bangs framed your

face, and you looked so gorgeous. My dick hated me all night long, but my heart was happy."

She smiles wickedly. "Well, at least you know your dick will be happy tonight."

I groan as I lean in and kiss her. "You have no idea what you do to me."

She rolls her body against mine. "Of course I do. Same thing you do to me. Light me on fire, fill my heart, and"—she drags her finger down my chest—"turn me on." She grazes her lips over mine, then turns away. "Come on, let's get some food."

I watch her hips sway in the belted mauve dress she's wearing and decide food can wait.

Catching up to her, I wrap my arm around her waist. "I have a better idea. Come on."

"Devon—what—where are we going?"

"Somewhere special," I tease, dragging her out of the ballroom and down the hallway toward the kitchen. Once in the kitchen, I lead her over to the pantry and pull her inside, shutting the door behind us.

I flick the light on and find Kennedy looking up at me, eyes dancing. "We need to find something to play spin the bottle with." Her voice is soft but sultry. She turns around and pretends to look over the shelves, before sighing, turning back around, and finally asking the question that set everything else off. "Do you really want to play spin the bottle?"

I move closer, looking deep into her eyes. "There's only one girl I really want to kiss."

"Oh? Who?"

I grab her arm, my gaze dropping to her lips as I say the word I was too chicken to say back then. "You." Then I crush my lips over hers. Our tongues collide in a frantic, needy kiss.

Walking her backward, I press her against the shelves and slide my hand along the bottom of her dress and up her thigh. She wraps her leg around my waist and tilts her hips toward me.

"What do you want, baby?" I ask, grazing my finger along the edge of her underwear before pushing it to the side and stroking her wet pussy.

"Fuck me. Right here. Right now."

Jesus fuck.

A second later, her fingers are on the waist of my pants, undoing the button and freeing my aching cock.

"What do *you* want?" she purrs.

"To fuck you. Right here." I drag my lips over her neck. "Right now."

"Then what are you waiting for?"

Holding her steady, I plunge inside her, groaning. I pause for a moment once I'm inside her because this is going to happen way too fast otherwise.

"Devon," she complains. "Move."

"Sorry, I need a second."

"No, you don't. This is a quickie. Hard. Fast. *Now.* Please."

"Please?" I ask, lips pressed into her neck.

"Please, baby. I need you. Make me come."

Fuck it.

Without another word, I drive into her hard and fast as she cries out.

She arches her back, pressing into me so I can get even deeper.

"Fuck," I groan, bracing one hand against the wall.

At the sound of footsteps in the kitchen, I go faster, and the thrill of being caught takes us both over the edge.

We're panting as I pull out and tuck my dick back in my pants. I give her a hard kiss and fix her underwear for her just as there's a knock on the pantry.

She quickly fixes her dress, then wipes some lipstick off my face before I open the door to see a couple of the girls who helped plan the reunion standing there.

"Need something?" I ask.

"Uh, more napkins," one says. She blinks a couple of times, then smiles. "Sorry if we *interrupted.*"

"Not at all. We were just looking for something to play spin the bottle with." Kennedy bites her lip and looks down, trying not to laugh. "Napkins are on the right. Take whatever you need," I say, taking Kennedy's hand and quickly leading her away.

AFTER ENJOYING some food from the potluck dinner, Kennedy and I are dancing on the dance floor set up in the corner by the DJ.

My fingers twist through Kennedy's hair as she leans against me, enjoying the slow song.

"I'm glad you made sure we went to all those dances together. They're some of my favorite memories," she whispers.

"Mine too. And camping in the backyard."

"Still more memories to be made doing that."

"Definitely. I'm so happy you're here, that you're staying. I feel like a kid on Christmas who got everything he wanted."

"Same," she breathes.

I hold her closer, feeling every sensation—how her weight shifts as she sways to the song, the way her chest touches mine as she breathes in, and how her breath tickles my neck when she breathes out. I take it all in, grateful and still in disbelief that she's in my arms. I'm going to revel in this feeling for as long as I can, because I never dreamed I'd get this lucky.

EPILOGUE
THREE MONTHS LATER

THEY WERE *a generation promised that they could have it all if they worked hard, but somewhere between that promise being made and their generation coming of age, the world changed. That promise was null and void as they hit adulthood and were left working long hours for little pay with crushing student loan debt piling up.*

I lean back in my chair, flexing and stretching my fingers as I reread what I've written. I recently pitched an article about careers, housing, finance, and lifestyle through the mid-1900s and early 2000s. It's been interesting so far, seeing how things have changed, especially the outlook on jobs and careers and what each generation values, and how the meaning of "hard work" has changed.

Millenials, as I wrote in my last paragraph, got the shit end of the stick. At least as Gen Z, we knew it was going to suck for us. Millenials still had hope.

I stand up from my chair and stretch, looking around the office. Before I moved in, it was a collection of boxes, scattered exercise equipment, and a small desk. Now the boxes are gone—what was inside them all sorted and organized in different places throughout the house. The exercise equipment is settled in one corner, and in the other corner, I have Sharon's old sewing table, which I've turned into a desk. I also bought an insanely comfortable chair, because I spend a fair amount of my time working in here.

After trying it out for a few weeks, I ended up loving running events at the inn. It turns out that's a great fit for me. Devon quickly put together an event coordinator position for me. It's still only part time because other than weddings and occasional local events, there's not much else going on. I'm hoping to increase the number of weddings held there over the coming year, so Devon and I have been working together to create a strong social media presence to drive people toward the inn. So far, it's been working.

I also pushed past the fears I had about pitching ideas to bigger online magazines and websites, and had a few accepted. This is my second big piece, and I'm really excited about it. In addition to those two things, I've still been volunteering at the library and helping Claire plan events at Bloom Beauty here and there. None of it is how I saw my career going, but I love it this way. I get to do all the things I enjoy without any of them burning me out, and I'm still making a living. But if my research for the article has taught me anything, it's that Gen Z likes to buck tradition—and often authority—when it comes to college and careers.

The doorbell rings, and I take that as a sign to take a break. My eyes were starting to feel fuzzy, and I'm already ahead of my word count goal for this week, anyway.

After turning off my computer, I head downstairs and open the door. The mail truck is down the road and there's a box on the porch. I excitedly drag it inside and take it into the living room before tearing it open.

What I see makes me smile. A bunch of signed books from indie author Jade Jackson. After reading all her books over the course of a couple of weeks, Justin slid into her DMs and they've had a whirlwind love story ever since. She and Justin both signed copies of one of her books—which they're working together to narrate—for the book club. There's a sticky note on one with my name on it.

I open it and look at the title page.

KEND,

HERE'S TO FALLING IN LOVE WITH YOUR BEST FRIEND. WE PICKED THIS ONE JUST FOR YOU.

LOVE YA,

JUSTIN

Below it is another signature from Jade.

Kennedy,

Can't wait till I get to meet you in person. Hope your book club loves this one. (And doesn't hate the cliffhanger! I promise to send the next if they want it.)

See you soon.

XO

Jade

I laugh at that. Justin and Jade will be coming out here for a visit in a couple of weeks when they have a reader event in the area. Though we've talked over text and video, I'm excited to finally meet Jade in person, especially since she's already met everyone else in our friend group. Frannie only lives a couple of towns over from her, and apparently Jade is a huge bandits fan, so Justin took her to a game.

"Hey, babe?" Devon calls through the back door. He's been working in the backyard all morning. We're so domesticated. I love it.

"Yeah?" I call, setting the book down and walking down the hall toward the kitchen.

He's smiling as he leans against the door, shirtless and hair mussed, looking like sex on a stick.

"Can you grab me some water?"

"Sure," I say, barely able to take my eyes off him for long enough to get some water for him. As I hand him the glass, his fingers brush mine and my core clenches. God, why is he so stupidly hot?

"Okay there?" he asks, grinning. "You look thirstier than me."

I take a deep breath, trying to calm my raging hormones. "Well, you sure know how to make a girl want to *sing.*"

He growls in response, and I'm about to climb him like a tree.

"Before we do *that,* come outside with me." I pout a little, but he smiles. "I promise, it's worth it." He extends his hand, and I take it without question.

I shut the door behind us as we step onto the back porch. As soon as we do, I see a section of the fence in the backyard set to look like a soccer goal.

"What is this?" I ask. "Is this what you've been doing all morning?"

"I mowed the yard first. Then raked the grass clippings so we wouldn't slip on them while we play. It's been too long. And since I know how much you love kicking soccer balls at a fence..."

I turn and throw my arms around his neck. "This is amazing." He leans in to kiss me, but I push away and run down the steps, grab the soccer ball, and dribble down the field toward the goal. A moment later, he's next to me and we're fighting for control of the ball. We both make shots at the goal and miss, but finally I get a good enough lead on him that I can take my time, and I manage to score.

He grins and runs for the ball as it rolls back to us, but when he gets close enough, he kicks too hard and it soars over the fence.

"Nice one," I tease. "Guess we better go get it." I stare over the fence, trying to see where it went.

"Actually, I have another," he says from behind me. The ball lightly hits the fence next to my feet. When I bend down to pick it up, I realize there's writing on it.

I turn it in my hand until the words are right side up. And, oh my god. It says...

Will you marry me?

I spin around to see Devon kneeling in front of me, ring box in hand.

"Kend, the day you moved in next door to me was the best day of my life. It's the day I met my partner in crime, my forever best friend, and the love of my life—even if I didn't know it at that moment. I'm so unbelievably lucky to have spent seventeen years as your best friend. Now I'm ready to spend the rest of my life as your husband. In many ways, nothing at all will change. It's still the same love, the same trust and respect we've always had for each other, but now it will grow in new, stronger ways as we walk through life together. I love you so much, Kennedy. Will you marry me?"

"Yes. Hell yes. All the fucking yeses. I love you."

He stands and wraps me in his arms, giving me a deep kiss. I lean into him, twisting my tongue with his until I remember...

"The ring!" I yell, leaning back.

He laughs and steps back, pulling the ring from the box and taking my hand. It's a gorgeous center cut diamond with small diamond clusters on either side set on a twisted platinum band. Classic and breathtaking.

"I love it."

"I'm glad. You have the most eclectic taste in jewelry. I had to get advice from Frannie and Hallie. And Claire went with me."

"You did good. It's perfect."

He kisses me again, then slowly pulls away before kissing my head and looking at me reverently.

"I can't wait to marry you."

"What are you thinking? Next week?" I tease.

"Maybe three weeks. Justin will be in town then. We'll just need to get the rest of your family from New York."

"I can't tell if you're serious or not."

"When it comes to marrying you, I'm always serious. Though it would be a lot to pull off that quickly."

"Well, I am the event planner at a gorgeous inn. I'm sure I could make it happen."

"Anytime, anywhere."

He sweeps me into his arms bridal-style and carries me toward the back porch, kissing me as he goes.

When I came back early for the reunion, I never could've predicted this is how it would end up, but in my heart, I know it's right. When I decided to stay, I told Devon I was smashing my window, carving out my own path, but really, I'd finally found the right one to walk, the right door to open. And it turns out I had the key the whole time. I just had to know where to look. I had to be honest about what I wanted and go for it.

Now I have it.

Who knew moving to Brighton seventeen years ago would end up being the best thing that ever happened to me?

Devon carries me up the stairs and into our bedroom, setting me on the bed, then climbing over the top of me.

"I love you," he whispers.

"I love you too," I breathe.

I may not have wanted to come here originally, but it turns out Brighton was always where I was meant to be. I just had to be willing to see that. Some people think fate controls every aspect of life, but I think there's a lot of free will involved, too. I'm thankful that I listened to my heart when it called me to the arms of my best friend. I'm even more thankful that I trusted my heart when it said I could have the future with him I always wanted.

Best decision ever.

The End

Grab a Kennedy & Devon bonus chapter, check out more of the Baker Girls series, sign up for Bethany's newsletter, and more here:

A NOTE FROM BETHANY

Thank you so much for reading Devon & Kennedy's story! I hope you enjoyed this fun little rom-com and all the teasing, flirting, and singing. ;)

If you want a little more fun and snarky banter, you can grab Devon & Kennedy's bonus chapter on my website.

Up next from the Baker Girls is Justin & Jade's marriage of convenience rom-com, *The Last Love Story*. And if you haven't yet, go back and check out Mark and Frannie's story in *The Last Lie*. Plus stay tuned for Hallie's story (*The Last Thing*) and Hardy & Ackley's story (*The Last Person*).

For more news, updates on what I'm working on, teasers, and freebies, sign up for my newsletter or hop over to my reader group, Bethany Monaco Smith's Book Besties

Thanks again for reading!
XO,
Bethany

BETHANY'S BOOKS

Freaking Love series
First Love
Real Love
Forever Love

Friends Like This series
Friends Like This
Falling Like This
Broken Like This
Love Like This
Married Like This
(a Friends Like This bonus novella)
Together Like This
Heartbreak Like This
Family Like This
Future Like This
Nothing Like This
Trust Like This
Always Like This

THE LAST KEY PLAYLIST

You can find the playlist for The Last Key on Spotify

- Heat of the Summer- Young the Giant
- Come To My Window- Melissa Etheridge
- There's No Way- Lauv, Julia Michaels
- I Don't Want To Be Friends- Jake Scott
- Dandelions- Ruth B.
- Always Been You- Jessie Murph
- In Case You Didn't Know- Brett Young
- Not Like I'm In Love With You- Lauren Weintraub
- Butterflies- MAX, FLETCHER
- One Of Them Girls- Lee Brice
- 18- One Direction
- Always Been You- Shawn Mendes
- Snow On The Beach- Taylor Swift, Lana Del Ray
- Nothing Like New York- Liddy Clark
- Stacy's Mom- Fountains Of Wayne
- Craving You- Thomas Rhett, Maren Morris
- Like No One Does- Jake Scott
- Here's to Us- Kevin Rudolf

- You Make It Easy- Jason Aldean
- A Thousand Years- James Arthur

ABOUT THE AUTHOR

Bethany Monaco Smith is a writer-mom. When she's not busy hanging with her boys, she's writing beautifully messy love stories.

She loves happily-ever-afters and cries at every emotional moment, whether reading, writing, or watching. When she's not mom-ing or writing, you can find her binge-reading on Kindle Unlimited, supporting fellow indie authors, and having sushi dates with her SIL. Bethany survives on coffee, rewatching the same TV shows over and over, and her KU subscription. She lives in the Southern Tier of NY with her husband and two sons.

For more about Bethany and what she's working on, follow along on Instagram or on her website, bethanymonacosmith.com. Stay in touch by joining Bethany's exclusive Facebook group, Bethany's Book Besties & signing up for her newsletter.

ACKNOWLEDGMENTS

Cassie, as usual, for being your incredible self. Thank you for listening to me complain, talking me off the ledge, and always being the organized one! I appreciate all your support and your friendship. XO

Lacey, thank you as always for the thoughtful edits, and more importantly your friendship. Love you!

The BOD squad for your endless support, cheering me on, and lifting me up. You are THE BEST. All the hearts.

To all my betas, thank you for your feedback and thoughts, and helping to make this story shine!

To my supremely awesome ARC/Street team, THANK YOU. You ladies are the absolute best and I could not do all this without you!

To the incredible author/bookish community I'm lucky to be a part of, thank you. You have been a source of camaraderie, support, and hilarious memes that keep me going on the rough days and celebrate with me on the awesome ones. Y'all are the best!

Finally, to all of you for picking up this book, reading this story, and (if you've read this far) hopefully falling in love with these characters. I appreciate every one of you!